E.Y.E. OF THE SCORPION
E.Y.E. Spy Mystery #1

CHERYL KAYE TARDIF

E.Y.E. OF THE SCORPION
E.Y.E. Spy Mystery #1

Copyright © 2016 by Cheryl Kaye Tardif. All Rights Reserved.

No part of this publication may be reproduced, stored in a retrieval system, or transmitted, in any form or by any means, electronic, mechanical, photocopying, recording, or otherwise, without prior written permission from the author.

This is a work of fiction. Names, characters, places and incidents either are the product of the author's imagination or are used fictitiously. And any resemblance to actual persons, living, dead (or in any other form), business establishments, events, or locales is entirely coincidental.

www.cherylktardif.com

FIRST EDITION Trade Paperback

September 15, 2016

Published by Imajin Qwickies®, an imprint of Imajin Books®

www.ImajinQwickies.com

ISBN: 978-1-77223-278-3

Cover designed by Ryan Doan: www.ryandoan.com

Chapter One

The Grim Reaper often came knocking when it was unexpected. That was something Eileen Edwards had figured out years ago. So when the phone on her desk rang at just after eight in the morning on Sunday, February 8th, she knew it wouldn't be good news.

"Call from Law-ree Nor-man," the androgynous call display voice told her.

Constable Larry Norman was a detective in Vancouver's Gang Task Force—and her former partner.

Eileen picked up the phone and grimaced as a twinge of pain shot through her right hand. "Sorry I can't come to the phone right now. Please leave your name and—"

"Really, Eileen? Is that the best you can do?"

"—after the beep. *Beeeep.*"

There was a slight pause. Then Larry said, "You done?"

She sighed and adjusted her reading glasses. "I hope this is a crank call."

"I need a favor. I need you to find a street kid named Zipper."

"You do know this is Family Day weekend *and* my first weekend off in forever."

"But you're already up and working anyway," Larry said.

Eileen leaned back in the chair and glanced across the room. The white letters on the glass door of the office reminded her that *E.Y.E. Spy Investigations* had bills to pay. "How do you know? Maybe you woke me."

Larry chuckled. "You're in your office. I can hear your printer gasping for breath in the background."

She glared at the hefty, aging machine that was busy groaning and vomiting up paper like Linda Blair puking up pea soup. Maybe the printer needed an exorcism.

Papers scattered on the floor told her she'd forgotten to extend the catch tray again. Another sheet shot out, and she caught it before it hit the floor with the others.

"You know, you should really trade that antique in for a modern printer," Larry said. "Maybe one built after 1990."

"It works fine. Now what's so important about this Zippy kid?"

"Zipper."

"What did he do—kill someone?"

"No, the opposite. We think he witnessed a murder."

"Poor kid." She sighed. "What do you know about him?"

"Not much. He's about fourteen. No priors. His mother is dead. Father unknown. He's not a big kid—wears a Canucks cap and gets around by skateboard."

Eileen scribbled notes on the back of the paper. "What's his real name?"

"No idea. He was raised by the street. Everyone calls him Zipper."

She frowned. "Is he a prostitute?"

"No. He's just fast on a skateboard."

"Then they should have called him Zippy. Tell me about the murder."

"You know I'm not supposed to talk

about an active GTF investigation."

"I need to know what I'm dealing with."

"Okay," Larry said, lowering his voice, "but you didn't hear this from me."

"Hear what?"

There was a brief pause before he spoke again. "There was a gang hit on Thursday around 2:00 a.m."

"Any casualties?"

"One body. Chen Li, a full-patch member of the Silver Scorpions."

"Guess Li will be riding Hell's highway now."

The Silver Scorpions Motorcycle Club was a multiracial gang that ran illegal narcotics up and down the west coast. It wasn't unusual to see a convoy of intimidating riders wearing black leather vests with the silver-on-red colors and silver scorpion logo on the back as they cruised south on Highway 99.

"What was Li's rank?" she asked.

"He *was* Pablo Alvarez's VP."

A few years ago Eileen had a run-in with Alvarez, the president of the SSMC. The man had a violent temper. "Alvarez must be pissed off losing his vice president and right-hand man."

"Oh, he's more than pissed off, Eileen. Alvarez is dead too. Fell down a flight of stairs just over a week ago. The Scorpions kept his death under wraps. Literally. Yesterday a health inspector found him buried in a crate of tortillas in the storage room at Mama Mia's Casa."

"Ugh. Remind me never to eat there."

"With Alvarez dead—"

"—Li moved from vice president to president," she finished.

"You got it. Except Chen Li's reign came with an early expiration date."

"So who's inherited the gavel now?"

"We have no idea."

"Where was Li found?"

"In an alley just off East Hastings Street. I'll text you the address."

"How did he die?"

"Two bullets to the head. Word on the street is that Li was executed by a rival gang over a shipment of botched counterfeit casino chips. Everything points to the Indie Warriors. We're interviewing two of their prospects now."

"You think an IW killed Li to get a patch?"

"You know how these MC initiations

work. Prospects have to prove their loyalty and worth."

"Are you expecting blowback from the Scorpions?"

"Retaliation is always possible. If there's a gang war brewing in Vancouver, we need to stop it before innocent people get caught in the crossfire."

Eileen couldn't agree more. "What makes you think this Zipper kid saw Li go down?"

"Zipper hangs out in that area. There's a bookstore two buildings down from where Chen was killed. The owner of the store often gives Zipper old books to read. Problem is, no one's seen the kid in days."

"Since the killing," she guessed.

"Exactly. Intel says he's on the run. And he won't last long without our protection."

"If I take this case," she said, "you'll owe me big."

"Thanks, Eileen."

"Thank me when I find the kid."

"I'll do that. By the way, no one else at the department knows I've called you in to locate him."

"Got it. One more thing, Larry."

"What's that?"

"Since it's my day off, I'm billing you for today. Double time."

Eileen hung up the phone and stared down at the scribbled notes, contemplating what Zipper must have done to survive. Drug trafficking, theft, prostitution—those were only three possibilities out of many.

The slithering underbelly of Vancouver had calcified scales, while its half-hidden face had razor-sharp fangs that injected a devious poison of hopelessness into its prey. Survival of the fittest reigned supreme on the streets. Most long-term runaways ended up joining one of the prominent gangs like the Silver Scorpions, which were responsible for the city's drug and prostitution problems. No one living on the streets of the city was immune to the seduction of a street gang posing as a motorcycle club and replacement family.

A decade ago the Demonios de Los Muertos (DLM) had sauntered north of the US border, smuggling hardcore military-grade weapons into Canada. There were even whispers that the Scorpions and DLM were negotiating a merge. Then there were the Indie Warriors, which consisted of various First Nations bands. The IW laundered dirty money for the other gangs through the casinos.

As a former police officer and now a private investigator, Eileen knew all about the part of the city most tourists never saw—the ugly and often deadly part. They saw the beauty of the ocean and mountains, but they complained about the traffic and the rain.

Removing her reading glasses, she tucked them into her blouse pocket and peered out the window. A dismal gray stained the winter sky, as though someone had thrown a can of watery paint into the air. A few splatters of rain hit the windowsill, but mostly the moisture clung to the ashen clouds, expanding by the minute like some kind of alien mold. It would pour later, probably when most inconvenient. Like rush hour.

She drew in a deep breath. Then she rose from the chair, locked the glass door that led outside and headed toward a second door at the far end, which deposited her in the living room of the three-bedroom Coquitlam bungalow she'd bought with Frank almost seventeen years ago. During the divorce, she'd fought to keep her home. It held too many memories, and she couldn't find the courage to move away, even though some of those memories were painful.

She shook her head. *Don't think of that now.*

Her gaze drifted across the massive room with its semi-open floor plan, "semi" because of the narrow wall featuring a wood-burning fireplace that stood between the living room and the kitchen. At the far end, wall-to-wall windows overlooked a lush backyard. Above her, a vaulted ceiling with a cedar beam ran along the peak, and a ceiling fan dangled from a brass cord in the center. To her right, the granite kitchen counters gleamed in various shades of sand and gold. The walls were pale beige, with a hint of peach. The warm color carried through to the rest of the house, except for two rooms. Her bedroom at the end of the hall was a pale aqua.

"Sand and ocean," she'd told the painters when she'd repainted the interior. Since she couldn't afford a house with an ocean view, she'd created her own beach world, her sanctuary.

She strode to the kitchen island and made a cup of chai tea. She never drank coffee anymore. She had enough bitterness in her life without assaulting her taste buds too.

Settling into the chocolate-colored leather couch, she sipped her tea and listened to the music that wafted through the speakers below the flat-screen television Larry had bought her as a housewarming gift. She'd argued with him that it was too expensive a gift, but he'd insisted.

Now if she could only figure out how to use the remote control. Apparently she had a PVR too, if only she could figure out how to record her shows on it. There was another remote for that. When the Shaw guy had installed it, he'd spent ten minutes explaining how the machine worked. In one ear and out the other. No matter how hard she tried, anything to do with technology simply didn't stick, and since she couldn't figure out how to do anything other than watch TV, she used the music channels instead of the stereo that Larry had kindly programmed into the TV remote control.

Something buzzed beside her. Her cell phone. It was a six-year-old LG model with text. Nothing fancy like kids had these days. What did she need with FacePlace or whatever it was called? And that Tweety thing everyone did? Who needed all those distractions?

Larry's text message had arrived, and she made a face when she read the address. Not a part of the city she liked to be in.

She checked her watch. 8:48.

Downing the remainder of the tea, she let out a sigh then stood. It was time to go find a missing kid.

What was his name again? Zippy?

Chapter Two

It took her over an hour of dodging traffic and jaywalkers, and cursing all the Sunday drivers who should be at home or confessing their sins at church, but finally Eileen reached the alley where the shooting had taken place. She slowed her Honda Civic, which a previous—and obviously color-blind—owner had painted what could only be described as rotten avocado. The car had seen better days. Hell, it had seen better decades, the rust outweighing the paint by about two-thirds, but she couldn't afford to buy a new vehicle, much less fix the piece of junk she already owned.

Parking behind a cigar shop, she cut the engine. Retrieving the baton and can of pepper spray she kept in the glove box, she exited the car and surveyed the alley. Next to the cigar shop was Tai-Wan-On, the Taiwanese restaurant where Li had taken his last breath. Beside the restaurant sat Crowley's Books. A tattoo parlor was at the far end.

"Okay, crime scene," she muttered, "show me what you've got."

Yellow police tape that had been used to cordon off the area four days ago was now wrapped around fence posts, the loose ends fluttering in the breeze. A light sprinkle of rain that morning had played havoc with some of the evidence, but two bullet holes in a graffiti-covered Dumpster behind the Tai-Wan-On restaurant told her that Chen Li was a very short man if he'd been hit in the head.

Unless Li's killer had made him get down on his knees.

She wondered if Larry had thought of that or if it even mattered.

"You gonna stare at dat Dumpster all day, Miss Eileen?" a hoarse voice called out.

Eileen smiled at a bone-thin black woman pushing an overloaded shopping cart toward her. Alfie was a common sight around Granville Island, and she'd been one of Eileen's confidential informants back when Eileen was with VPD. No one knew Alfie's full name or her age. Eileen guessed the woman was somewhere around eighty, but she never was good at judging ages.

"How come you're not in your usual neighborhood, Alfie?"

"Gotta go where de action is."

"I see you have a new cart."

Alfie gave her a toothless grin. "I 'herited it from Ole Pete after he passed."

"He was one of the good guys."

"Ole Pete was a war hero. Fought in dem wars over in de desert."

Pete Hutchins, former officer in the Canadian Armed Forces, had never recovered from his frequent tours to Iraq and Afghanistan. He'd watched several of his comrades explode into a million pieces and witnessed countless horrific atrocities. Upon his return to Canada, he was diagnosed with PTSD. Not long after an honorable discharge from the military, Pete ended up on the streets, unable to hold down a job or provide for his wife and children. Drugs came next—anything to numb the pain of loss and halt the memories of lives snuffed out prematurely.

Eileen understood the desire to escape that kind of pain.

"Are you here 'bout dat murder?" Alfie asked.

"What do you know about it?"

"Not much, hon. Only what I heard 'round town."

"What are people saying?"

"Dem gangs are gonna kill each other."

Maybe we should let them. "Anyone taking credit for the hit?"

"Not dat I heard. But I keep an ear out, if you want."

"I appreciate it."

One thing she knew about Alfie, the woman might be dancing the two-step with Death, but she was a fighter. And she noticed things, stuff others would shrug off.

"You gonna ask me 'bout dat boy?"

"You know about Zippy?"

Alfie nodded. "*Zipper.* I took him in. Bin lookin' after him last two weeks."

"So he up and left without a word to you?"

"Yup. Cooked him dinner, then he went walkin'. That was four nights past. Never came back. Didn't even take his belongin's.

Got 'em here." Alfie patted the plastic sheet that protected the objects in her cart. "Wanna see?"

"Definitely. I need to locate Zipper, especially if he witnessed the shooting."

"He in danger?"

"Could be. If you know where he is, Alfie, you need to tell me."

"Don't know where he gone or if he be back." She rummaged around in her cart, while Eileen waited patiently. "Here's his bag." Alfie lifted the grimy object. "Blue elves or somethin' on it."

"Smurfs." Eileen gingerly accepted the backpack, which screamed of youth and innocence.

The front pocket contained three hotel pens, two pencils and a ratty spiral notebook filled with sketches of local buildings and street people. Eileen recognized one of a slumbering Alfie, the woman's wrinkled face softened by sleep. The kid had talent.

She tucked the notebook back into the pocket and opened the center section. There wasn't much inside—a water bottle, a toothbrush, a picture of a beer bottle ripped from a magazine, half a package of chewing gum, a beat-up paperback of *The*

Neverending Story and a cloth pouch holding a tensor bandage, a rolled-up pair of mismatched socks and a washcloth. Inside the toe of one of the socks, she discovered a battered Sucrets tin with twenty-four dollars in bills and a handful of change.

"Did you show this backpack to the police?"

"Cops didn't ask to see it." Alfie winked. "So I kep' it for you."

"How'd you know I'd be here?"

"Your pal Larry tol' me you'd be asking questions 'round here. An' here you be."

Eileen raised a brow. "Guess I'm too predictable."

"Dat's what *he* said."

"Have any idea what Zipper's real name is?"

Alfie shook her head. "Only ever knowed him as Zipper. If he got a real name, he never told me."

"And he's fourteen?"

"Dat's what he told Ole Pete. Zipper didn't talk much 'bout hisself. A shy one too, dat boy. Don't trust no one neither. You be gentle-like when you find him." Alfie stared off into the distance. "Kid like dat shouldn't be livin' dis life."

"No one should." Eileen pulled a fifty-dollar bill from her jacket pocket. "Here. Lunch is on me."

"Thank you, hon. You're a sweet girl."

Eileen was hardly a "girl." She was nearing forty-nine and not happy about it. "Make sure you find a shelter tonight. It's going to be a cold one."

"I gots me a warm place over by de car wash, so don't you be worryin' 'bout me. This ole girl can take care of herself." Alfie rasped out a laugh that ended in a ragged cough.

"Don't you go spending all that on smokes." Eileen nodded to the money clenched in Alfie's fist. "You need food. And don't show anyone that money."

Alfie pushed her cart another few feet then stopped and looked over one frail shoulder. "Check out dat ole bowling alley. One dat burned down. You know it?"

"Liberty Lanes?"

"Kids hang 'round dat place day an' night. Zipper might be hangin' wit 'em."

"Why didn't you tell Constable Norman that?"

"Who?"

"Larry. You could've told him."

Alfie shrugged. "Like I said, Zipper's skittish. Figured you'd have a better chance gettin' him to come home. An' if de boy *did* see somethin' dat night, I knew you'd take care of him. You will, right?"

"Yeah."

"Go on now, Miss Eileen. Dis a dangerous place for a cop."

"I'm not a cop anymore, remember?"

"No, you *much* more." Alfie's gaze pierced her soul. "You care 'bout us. Not many do." The woman ambled off, her shopping cart rattling over potholes and loose gravel.

Eileen slung the Smurf backpack over one shoulder and headed back to her car. She was somewhat disappointed that no one had stolen it while she was preoccupied with Alfie. One day she might do what Larry always suggested—leave the keys in the ignition and attach a sign that read: *FREE CAR.*

Eileen tossed the backpack on the duct-taped passenger seat and drove off, the Honda burping up coils of charcoal smoke behind it.

Her cell phone rang, and she answered it without looking at the screen. "What do you want now, Larry?"

"How about a little somethin' somethin' on the side?" a low voice said. This was followed by a burst of feminine laughter.

"Very funny, Bobbi."

Bobbi Hathaway had been her best friend since high school. She and her husband, Rusty, often came over for dinner, back when Eileen and Frank were still together. They rarely came over as a couple anymore, but when Eileen needed a girl's night out—or in—Bobbi usually came by with a bottle of wine and a pair of pajamas.

"You really should check to see who's calling before you answer," Bobbi warned. "I could have been a psycho serial killer."

"You *are*! I saw the way you packed away the Cheerios last time you stayed over."

"Ha ha. Very punny."

"Puns aside, I feel like I've run a marathon, my joints ache so badly."

"Anyone stay over last night?"

"Nope. It was just me, myself and I. We had a party."

"And you didn't invite me? I'm hurt. Especially since Rus is out of town this weekend."

"I don't think you would've enjoyed yourself."

"Ah, one of those famous Eileen Edwards pity parties. Yeah, I'd rather stay at home with the boys and listen to them argue about who can burp and fart the loudest."

"Come on by tonight after supper, and we'll catch up."

"How about now?"

"Sorry, Bobbi, I'm in the middle of—"

"—a case. I know. Where are you headed this time? Downtown to spy on a philandering socialite?"

"Bowling alley," Eileen said. "I have a few 'pins' to knock down."

Chapter Three

A few blocks south of the crime scene, Liberty Lanes was a testament to the impenetrable strength of brick and concrete buildings of days gone by. Five and a half years ago, after a fire had gutted the place, the city had condemned the building, even though all four walls still stood. Doors and windows were boarded up, and the once-red brick exterior had mutated into a deep shade of soot.

It was a shame, really. No more 5-pin or 10-pin bowling tournaments. No more glow-in-the-dark bowling for the neighborhood kids. No more random hookups and used condoms in the back room behind the lanes. No more drug deals in the alley, or at the shoe rental counter.

"Yeah, I know this place," Eileen murmured as she pulled into the overgrown weed garden that was once the parking lot.

The ruins stood forlorn and forgotten, a relic of a different time. And speaking of time, the owner was doing plenty of it. He was locked away on fraud charges. The stupid guy had set the fire intentionally, hoping to get the insurance money—except he'd reneged on the last three payments, and his policy had been voided.

The Liberty Lanes fire had been one of Eileen's final cases before she'd traded her badge, Taser and gun for a business card, a baton and her Canon camera. She still had a gun, though not a standard service weapon like the .40 caliber Sig Sauer P226 she used to carry. As a former police officer with weapons training and a certified investigator with security papers, she was eligible to get a permit for a handgun, though she didn't carry it on the job. A lightweight Ruger LC9 was locked away in a gun safe in the nightstand beside her bed, but she'd never fired it. Fact is, she hadn't fired a gun since—

A sharp rap on the driver's side window

made her turn her head. Staring back at her was a kid in his mid-teens, with spiked jet-black hair, neon blue eyelashes and black lips sporting two snake-bite crystal studs. He straddled a ten-speed beside the car, and under one arm he held a skull-embossed skateboard.

Eileen rolled down the window. "Can I help you?"

"You lost, lady?" More piercings glimmered in his ears and brows.

"Nope. I'm exactly where I'm supposed to be."

The kid flicked a nervous look over his shoulder. "You shouldn't hang around here. It's not a safe neighborhood. Besides, the place is condemned."

She smiled. "I'm well aware of that fact."

The kid squinted at her. "You a cop?"

"Nope."

"You looking to score some drugs?"

She raised a brow at him. "Do I look like I want drugs?"

"Because if you are," he quickly added, "I don't deal."

"I'm looking for someone."

"Can't help you there."

"I haven't told you who I'm looking for."

The kid raised both hands, including the one grasping the board. "Don't know anything. I swear."

"What's your name?"

"Spence."

She blinked in surprise. "Really? I would've thought you'd have some cool nickname like Spike."

"Spence *is* my nickname. Listen, lady, I've gotta head out." His gaze drifted toward the ruins.

Eileen gave the door a nudge with her shoulder as she opened it. "What's the rush? You just got here. Besides, there might be something in it for you."

As she climbed out, Spence backed away. "I don't do old broads."

She let out a frustrated groan. "And I don't do little boys. I'm talking cash for information."

Interest piqued in the kid's eyes. "What kind of information?"

"I'm a private investigator, and I've been hired by a friend to find a missing kid. He's a few years younger than you, rides his skateboard around here and wears a Canucks cap."

Spence shook his head. "Haven't seen him."

"Maybe we should ask your friends inside."

Blue lashes flared. "What? There's no one in there. Place is locked up tighter than a virgin's pu—"

"Purse! I know that's what you were about to say."

With a shrug, Spence began to walk the bike backwards. "Lady, I haven't seen Zipper in days. No one has."

She marched over to him. "I didn't say his name was 'Zipper,' did I?"

Spence shrugged. "I know the kid. Last time I saw Zipper he was counting change for the bus."

"When was that?"

"The night of the shooting."

"Where would he take the bus to?"

"How the hell would I know?" Blue-lashed eyes rolled heavenward. "Do I look like his freakin' travel agent?"

Eileen grabbed Spence's shirt. "Listen, jerk-off, there are some really bad people looking for Zipper. I'm *not* one of them, but I can get nasty if I have to." She yanked her baton from its harness and waved it in front of his face. "So if you know anything, you'd better tell me.

"Fine! The park."

"Which park?"

"Stanley. Zipper calls it his 'retreat.' Goes there a couple times a week."

"Where exactly?"

"I don't know, but he meets a girl there."

"The girl have a name?"

Spence let out an exaggerated sigh. "All Zipper said was she sits on a rock and stares at the ocean. He watches her. The kid's a bit of a perv, if you ask me."

Eileen released her grip and smoothed his shirt. "See? That wasn't too difficult." She handed him a business card. "If you see him, call me. Immediately. Got it?"

"Sure."

She climbed back inside her car.

"Wait!" Spence yelled. "Aren't you gonna pay me?"

"Who said anything about money?" She started the engine.

"You said you'd give me something.'"

"Oh that."

Spence actually smiled. "So I get a reward for the information?"

"Yup. I won't tell the police you and your friends are hanging out in a condemned building. That's your reward."

She sped away, leaving the kid in a cloud of smoke and weeds.

Chapter Four

Eileen knew exactly where she'd find Zipper. Spence had given her the clue when he'd told her Zipper liked to stare at a girl who sat on a rock all day. There was only one place in Stanley Park where someone would have that kind of view.

The famous Seawall path was paved and traveled the circumference of the park, offering over five and a half miles of spectacular views. Usually the place was packed with people either walking or on bikes, skateboards or rollerblades. Today the park was sparsely dotted with nature lovers. It was too damned cold.

Strolling down the Seawall path, she shivered at the chilly air that skimmed off the ocean, wishing she'd stayed in her warm car. Occasional salty gusts slapped her in the face, and she gritted her teeth, wondering if Mother Nature was trying to tell her something. She pushed on.

She thought of what she'd say to Zipper. If he *had* seen anything the night of the shooting, the kid was in danger. No killer liked having a witness, much less one that was still alive and could start squealing any minute. She had to convince him to come in off the streets.

She spotted a petite figure on a skateboard up ahead. Dressed in jeans, an oversized black hoodie and winter boots that had to be at least two sizes too big, he was doing tricks on his board. Even with the layers of clothing, she could tell one thing for sure. The kid was scrawny; it was amazing he'd survived this long on his own.

Zipper did a final jump, kicked the board with the toe of his boot and caught it in one hand. Then he walked to the edge of the Seawall, propped the board up against the lip of the curb and jumped over the side. The tide was coming in, but one of the larger rocks was still within reach. He climbed atop it and sat down.

Eileen approached cautiously. The last thing she wanted was for the kid to run. She was too old to chase after him. She paused a few feet away from where Zipper had left his skateboard. He hadn't seemed to notice her. With a quiet grunt, she eased her butt down onto the curb and swung her legs over the Seawall.

Zipper looked over his shoulder at her. Under the ball cap, dark, uneven bangs hung low over eyes. He didn't say a word, but she could sense he considered her an intrusion.

"Girl in Wetsuit," she said with a smile.

The kid blinked. "Huh? You talking to me?"

She nudged her head toward the statue on the rock. "The statue is called 'Girl—'"

"I know, lady. I can read." Zipper snapped his gaze back to the statue and muttered something she couldn't make out.

Smart-ass. "Did you know it was inspired by the famous Little Mermaid statue in Copenhagen?"

The kid was silent.

Eileen smiled, triumphant. "People come from all over the world to see her, to admire her beauty."

"You talk like she's alive," Zipper said

without turning.

"Isn't she?"

For a long moment, they stared at the statue on the rock and watched the tide creep up the shore, swallowing other rocks in its path.

"This is a great place to hang out," she said.

Zipper shrugged. "It's okay."

"I like to call it my retreat."

His head whipped around. "You a cop?"

She smiled. "No." *Not anymore.*

"I have to go," Zipper said as he slid off the rock, his boots splashing in the water.

As he climbed over the wall a few feet away, she said, "I'm not a cop, but I *am* here to help you, Zipper."

"I don't need your help." He eyed the skateboard by her feet.

"If I could find you, so can whoever killed that guy in the alley."

That stopped the kid dead in his tracks.

Eileen stood up. "I can help you. That's why I'm here."

Zipper strode toward her and bent down to retrieve his board. "And how do you plan to help me? Put me in a foster home?"

Eileen frowned. She hadn't thought that

far ahead. Larry hadn't told her what they'd do with the kid once she located him. Besides, it was the long weekend, not the easiest time to dump a kid into emergency foster care.

Ah, shit, Larry.

"I'm not living with strangers," Zipper said. "No thanks, lady."

"I don't blame you."

"Anyway, I didn't see nothing that night."

"*Any*thing."

"Huh?" Zipper stared at her as if she were something he'd found rotting in the bottom of a Dumpster.

"'I didn't see *any*thing,' otherwise it's a double negative—"

"Jesus, lady. What are you—the grammar police?" Zipper spun on his heel and walked away.

"The problem is," she called after him, "whoever killed Chen Li thinks you *did* see something."

Zipper froze. As she caught up to him, he said, "You think they'll come here?"

"If they want you bad enough." She didn't like scaring the kid. His pale face proved he was already imagining what could happen to him. "This would be an easy place to dump a body, Zipper."

He took a step closer. "If you're not a cop, who are you?"

"Eileen Edwards, Private Investigator, at your service." She handed him a business card. "I was hired by the VPD to find you before Li's enemies did. So if you know who killed him, you need to tell me so the police can arrest him."

"I didn't see...*any*thing."

Her eyes narrowed as she studied the kid. He was lying. Okay, so he didn't trust her. She doubted he trusted anyone. She couldn't blame him.

Two men in identical black trench coats emerged from one of the central paths. They were too far away to make out any facial features. Eileen couldn't be sure, but they seemed to be surveying the area as though looking for someone.

Her inner alarm bells blared. "Damn."

"What's wrong?"

"We've got company coming, and not the Martha Stewart kind."

The kid shivered. "Can't we just go the other way?"

Eileen shook her head. "That would be

too obvious. No, we're going to walk right past them."

"Are you crazy, lady?"

"Shh, they'll hear you. Quick! Tuck your skateboard under your hoodie, and take off your cap."

Zipper followed her first instruction only.

"Cap," she repeated.

"I don't ever take it off. It's my lucky cap."

She sighed. "Fine. Pull the hood up. Now, make like you're my kid, and we'll both get out of here alive."

"Yes...*Ma*."

She flinched, but kept walking.

"I don't know what to do," Zipper whispered.

"Just follow my lead. And don't forget to smile."

The men were closing in on them.

"We'd better hurry home, Will," Eileen said in a loud voice. "Dad's going to wonder where we are."

"Uh, okay," Zipper said, his voice a bit shaky.

The men were a few feet in front of them now. They were arguing.

"Did you remember to do your homework, Will?" Eileen said, her gaze briefly resting on one of the men. "Good morning, gentlemen."

Neither men said a word as they passed, but she could feel their eyes burning into her back.

"Can we go to McDonald's for breakfast first, Ma?" Zipper said.

"Sure."

Eileen and her young charge made it to the parking lot without being accosted or slaughtered.

She unlocked the car doors. "Your backpack is on the front seat."

Zipper opened the passenger door, withdrew his skateboard from beneath his hoodie and climbed inside the car. "How'd you get my backpack? From the cops?"

"From Alfie," she said as she slid into the driver's seat and started the engine.

As they pulled out of the parking lot, Zipper said, "You know Alfie?"

"Yeah, we go way back."

Zipper's expression was doubtful. "You investigate her with your P.I. business?"

"No. We help each other out from time to time."

The kid mentally chewed on that bit of information.

Eileen felt safer once they were in traffic. A few glances at the vehicles behind her told her they weren't being followed. She knew all the tricks. It was part of her job, knowing how to see things without being seen. Even as a cop, she'd always been good at surveillance, and patience always paid off.

They drove in silence until they reached a strip of fast food restaurants.

"There's a McDonald's up ahead on the right," Zipper hinted.

"You do realize that was part of our little act, don't you?"

Zipper pouted and crossed his arms.

Eileen heard a slow rumble and realized it was the kid's stomach. Taking pity on him, she pulled into the right lane and took a sharp turn into the McDonald's parking lot. The drive-thru only had two cars ahead of her, so she pulled into the line.

"Can't we go inside?" Zipper asked.

She shook her head. "The less you're seen, the better. Just keep your head down."

While Zipper sulked in the seat beside her, she pulled the Honda up to the side window. She placed an order for a sausage and egg breakfast sandwich and a large double-cream tea. "What do you want?" she asked Zipper.

"Same, but with coffee."

She frowned. "Kids your age shouldn't…" Her voice faded as she caught his scornful gaze. She ordered the coffee.

Minutes later their breakfast was handed to them, and she pulled the car back onto the highway. Zipper pulled out a sandwich and set it on the center console for her. Then in a flurry of paper wrapper, he devoured his sandwich in mere seconds.

"How was it?" she asked.

"Awesome," he said, chewing noisily.

"When was the last time you ate?"

"Depends. You talking real food like this or 'Dumpster Delight,' as Alfie calls it?"

She shuddered. "Real food."

"Don't remember."

How sad that a teenaged boy couldn't remember his last decent meal.

He eyed her sandwich, still in its wrapper. "You gonna eat that?"

"No, you can have it."

The wrapper went flying, and the

sandwich was downed in five bites.

She chuckled. "I wasn't going to change my mind, you know."

"Never know."

She took a long swig of tea. Alfie was right. The kid didn't trust anyone.

They entered the boundary heading into Coquitlam.

"Hey...*Ma*," Zipper said. "Where exactly are you taking me? Social Services? P.I. Prison?" He snickered.

"The only place I know that's safe, smart-ass."

Chapter Five

When Eileen pulled into her driveway, Zipper noticed the sign on the glass door. "This is where you work?"

"And my home. It used to have three garages, but I closed one in for my business."

"Cool."

She parked the car in the double garage. "Be careful getting out. It's a little tight on your side."

Zipper opened the passenger door, and Eileen hissed in a breath as it almost hit the tarp-covered hulk that sat in the second garage.

"What's that?" he asked, eyeing the navy tarp.

"Never mind about that," she said, hustling him up the stairs and into the house. "Don't move. I need to turn off the security system." The system control panel was within reach. She typed in the code, her back to the kid. "Okay. Now we're ready."

Zipper took two steps forward, but she held up a hand. "Boots off. You can put your skateboard by the closet so I don't trip over it."

He dropped the skateboard on the floor, and Eileen flinched. "Take it easy, kid. I don't need dents in the floor."

Zipper said something unintelligible and set the backpack on the floor next to his board. Then he kicked off his boots, exposing damp threadbare socks that left wet marks on the tiled floor.

"I'll get you some dry socks."

"I'm good," Zipper replied, his jaw clenched tight.

"Come in, and sit down." She headed for the kitchen. "Want some tea?"

"Tea's for old—" Zipper closed his mouth when she turned and shot him a scowl. "You got any coke?"

"How about some apple juice?"

The kid sighed and flopped onto the

couch. "Yeah, whatever."

She eyed his filthy jeans and stained hoodie. "We need to do some laundry. I'll find you something you can wear while we wash those clothes of yours."

Zipper sat up, crossing his arms. "I said I'm good."

"You might be, but that's a new couch you're sitting on, and I didn't get it stainguarded. No arguments. Clean clothes will make you feel better." *And smell better too.*

Zipper snatched up the remote control and turned on the television. "You got cable?"

"Yeah."

"Netflix?"

"What's that?"

Zipper snorted. "If you don't know, you don't got it."

The kid was starting to get on her nerves. "I'll go get those clothes."

When she returned a few minutes later, she handed Zipper a pair of jeans, a t-shirt and thick socks. "I think these jeans will do, though they might be a bit big. Let me know if you need a belt."

"You got a boy?"

Eileen sucked in a breath. "No."

"Where'd you—"

"You can change in the bathroom, second door on the left." She pointed to the door, then headed for the kitchen. "I'll get your juice."

After a quick call to VPD, where she left a brief message for Larry, she returned to the living room. Setting the juice on the coffee table, she carried her mug of tea to the armchair and sat down. She could hear water running in the bathroom. Perhaps she should suggest Zipper take a shower.

She was still unsure of her decision to bring the kid here, but what choice did she have? At least here she could keep an eye on him, keep him out of trouble.

The bathroom door opened, and Zipper stepped into the hall. His face was rosy and clean, though he still had the cap on, and he had a firm grip on the waistband of the jeans, which were at least two sizes too big. "I think I need that belt."

"Give me a second," she said, jumping to her feet and rushing past him.

Seconds later, she handed him a black leather belt.

"Looks new," Zipper said.

Ignoring his comment, she said, "I'm

going to throw your clothes in the wash, and then I have some calls to make. You can watch TV, okay?"

Zipper grinned. "I'm down with that." He sat down on the couch, picked up the remote and brought up a menu she'd never seen before. "Hey, you got On Demand. Can I watch a movie?"

She shrugged. "Sure." She had no idea what On Demand was, but it sounded harmless enough.

Retrieving Zipper's dingy castoffs from the bathroom floor, she gingerly shook them over the laundry room sink, checked the pockets, which were empty, and tossed everything into the washing machine. Adding an extra dose of detergent, she set the washer at the hottest setting. God only knew what was growing on the kid's clothing.

On her way to her office, she paused and watched Zipper for a minute or two until she was sure he wasn't going anywhere. He seemed immersed in the movie, some action flick with lots of gunfire. She doubted it was a Disney film.

Keeping the door wide open, she picked up the phone and called Child Services. As she suspected, their offices were closed for the long weekend. The voice message claimed there was a number she could call if it was an emergency, but she hung up. Even if the place was open, Zipper wouldn't be any safer there. They'd place him in some emergency care home, with no understanding of the danger the kid was in. No, she needed to listen to her gut and keep the kid close. At least until she discussed things with Larry.

She opened the file marked "Zipper" and updated her notes. After supper she planned on asking the kid if he was telling the truth when he said he hadn't seen anything. Somehow she didn't believe him. He was hiding something. *That* was evident by his occasional shifty eyes and expression.

Out in the living room, Zipper swore.

She glanced at her watch. It was nearly one, on her day off, and she'd already clocked a few hours. She marked the time on Zipper's file, closed and stamped it, *"Assignment completed."*

She called Larry's cell phone this time. He didn't pick up. *Now what to do?*

She left a message. "As I'm sure you know, Child Services is closed for the holiday. I'm going to bill you for every hour this kid is with me, Larry. Call me."

Exiting her office, she did the only thing she could do. She sat down with Zipper and watched a movie about some guy trying to rescue his daughter from terrorists. She recognized the actor. Liam something.

"He's gonna kill them all," Zipper said.

"Have you seen this already?"

The kid shook his head. "Naw, this is the fourth one, but they're all the same."

"If they're all the same, why bother watching it?"

Zipper shrugged. "It's cool to see the good guy win."

* * *

Larry called later that afternoon. "Excellent job finding our witness, Eileen."

"He claims he didn't see anything."

"Ah, but you know how to coax the information out of him. Gain his trust. You always were great at that. Brilliant, in fact."

"Don't try and butter me up," she said. "You know damned well I now have no choice but to let the kid stay with me until Tuesday."

Larry cleared his throat. "Aw, crap, I forgot it was a holiday weekend."

"Yeah, sure you did."

"Listen, I really do appreciate you helping us out and finding the kid. You're awesome."

"Yeah, yeah, yeah. You can kiss my butt another time. But come Tuesday morning, I want you on my doorstep with Child Services." She paused. "By the way, I found Zipper at Stanley Park, and there were two guys I'm sure were looking for him. And they weren't Indie Warriors."

"How do you know?"

"One was Asian, and the other was whiter than Mr. Clean."

"Silver Scorpions, maybe."

"Possibly."

"Doesn't surprise me, Eileen. If they think Zipper knows the identity of Li's killer, they're going to want to hand out their own kind of justice. Stay alert, Eileen. And for God's sake, keep him inside."

She peeked at Zipper, who had his eyes glued to the TV. "I don't think that'll be a problem."

After hanging up, she wandered from room to room, checking the window locks. The door to the garage had a deadbolt, and she slid it into place. She did the same with the front door and the door that led from the side of the house into her office.

"No one's getting in here."

"You say something, lady?" Zipper hollered.

"It'll be supper soon. You like pizza?"

"Who doesn't? Can we have pineapple on it?"

"Sure." She was somewhat surprised the kid liked his pizza the same way she did. Larry and Bobbi always teased her about her pizza choice.

When the pizza guy arrived, Eileen checked him out on the security system camera. White-haired male in his early sixties, she guessed. Grandpa was definitely *not* a gang member—unless the stars of *Cocoon* had formed one.

Fifteen minutes later, the large Hawaiian pizza was completely devoured, along with a bottle of 7-Up that went with it, while outside an evening storm moved in, adding a general gloominess to the evening.

"How about a game of poker?" Zipper said, holding up a tattered and stained deck of cards.

She frowned. "I'm not sure I want to touch those cards. Where have you been keeping them—in a Dumpster?"

Zipper gave her a sideways glance. "They're *your* cards."

"Just deal, kid. I have a container of pennies somewhere."

They were into their fourth game—none of which Eileen had won—when the doorbell rang. She went to the door and checked the camera, but all she could see was someone in a raincoat, his face obscured by a hood and rain.

"Go into the bathroom," she told Zipper. "Don't come out until I tell you."

The kid's eyes widened with fear, but he obeyed.

Eileen strode into her bedroom, opened the nightstand drawer and punched in the six-digit code for the gun case. Retrieving her handgun, she tiptoed to the door and checked the camera. Whoever had been out there was gone. She pressed a button, switching from the front door view to her office door.

There he is!

He jiggled the doorknob. Thank God she had locked it earlier.

Using the cameras positioned around her home, she watched the figure move stealthily around her house to the back door.

She tiptoed down the hall and into the storage room where the back door was located. The door had a peephole. Sucking in a deep breath, she slowly leaned forward and pressed her eye against the hole. The light above the door was out. Damn!

Suddenly an eye swooped in close to the peephole.

A hard knock sounded.

Eileen jumped, aiming the Ruger at the door. "I've got a gun!"

"Well, I've got a bottle of Arbor Mist," a voice yelled back.

"Oh Jesus," Eileen said as she quickly unbolted the door and ushered Bobbi inside. "I am so sorry. I completely forgot you were coming over tonight."

Bobbi's raincoat released a puddle of water onto the floor. "I can leave, if you want."

"No, you're staying." Eileen grabbed a towel from a shelf. "Here, dry off your face and hair."

"It's freezing out there."

"We'll put the fireplace on. I'll make some tea. The wine can wait until you've warmed up."

Bobbi kicked off her boots, shed the raincoat and hung it up on a hook then followed her down the hall. "Uh, can you put that thing away?"

Eileen tucked the gun into the waistband of her jeans. "Sorry."

"What's with the gun anyway?"

"I thought you were trying to break in."

Bobbi shivered.

"Go on in and sit down," Eileen said. "I'll make some tea."

Taking a detour into her bedroom, she locked the gun back in its safe and selected a sweatshirt from a drawer. She was halfway to the living room when she heard a shriek. Rounding the corner, she found Bobbi standing in the middle of the room.

"What's wrong?"

Bobbi pointed a shaky finger toward the couch. "You've got a...*boy*...in your house."

"Oh, right. This is Zipper. Zipper, this is my best friend, Bobbi." She handed Bobbi the sweatshirt. "Go in the bathroom and change your shirt. I'll fill you in after."

Bobbi made a beeline for the bathroom.

Zipper scowled at Eileen. "Your friend never seen a kid before?"

"Don't be a smart-ass. She was just startled, that's all."

The kid pulled his cap lower over his eyes. "Yeah, whatever."

Bobbi returned, her auburn hair still damp. "Thanks for the shirt, Eileen."

"Let's chat in the kitchen."

As Eileen passed Zipper, he whispered, "You gonna tell her about me? Why I'm here, I mean?"

Eileen nodded. "I trust her. You can too." She didn't tell the kid her friend was also a psychologist.

In the kitchen, she filled Bobbi in on her latest assignment.

"You sure this is a good idea?" Bobbi asked. "The kid could rob you blind."

"There's not much to steal. Besides, it's only for a couple of nights."

"You think he saw who killed Li?"

"I don't know."

"But he willingly came with you. That says something."

"Maybe he's just tired of street life and rummaging through other people's garbage for a meal."

Bobbi patted Eileen's hand. "Or he knows he's in danger, and he trusts you."

"I don't know why." Eileen shrugged. "I'm a complete stranger to him."

"Want me to talk to him?"

"As a psychologist?"

"He doesn't have to know that. Not yet."

They returned to the living room, where Zipper had fallen asleep on the couch. His facial features had softened, giving him an air of innocence. His thin arms hugged one of the oversized cushions, and Eileen could swear his eyelashes were damp.

"Poor kid," Bobbi said. "I can't imagine either of my sons surviving life on the street."

Eileen smirked. "They'd make it maybe four hours. They'd be back in time for supper."

"You know my kids so well."

"Let's let Zipper sleep. We've got a bottle of wine to polish off."

Back in the kitchen, they chatted until the wine was gone.

"I'm going to head home now," Bobbi said just before midnight.

"I thought you were staying over."

"You have enough company tonight."

After Bobbi left, Eileen retrieved a blanket from the linen closet, covered

Zipper and turned off the TV. She was tempted to remove his cap and set it on the coffee table, but he'd been so adamant about keeping it on, and she wanted to respect that. Besides, God only knew what lurked in his hair.

Standing over the kid, she watched him sleep. Freshly scrubbed and smelling of Bounce dryer sheets, he seemed so young and innocent. What a rough life he'd had, with not much to look forward to. How could anyone survive such a hopeless existence, much less a child? She felt a tug at her heart, a deep despair followed by yearning.

Leaving one lamp on, she headed down the hall. She paused briefly at the bedroom door that continued to taunt her, the door that hadn't been opened in years—until tonight. Pressing a palm against the door, she wondered what her life would have been like if that one night years ago had ended differently.

She swallowed hard, turned on one heel and entered her bedroom. Minutes later she slid beneath the duvet and stared up at the ceiling, while one thought played over and over in her mind.

Some doors are meant to stay closed.

Chapter Six

On Monday morning Eileen awoke to the sound of gunfire. She fumbled for her gun safe then realized her house guest was watching TV again.

Dressing, she wandered out to the living room. "Good morning, Zipper. How'd you sleep?"

The kid blinked a couple of times as though confused. "Uh, okay, I guess."

"Can you turn that down a bit? I haven't even had my morning tea."

"You got any coffee?"

"I think I have some instant somewhere."

In the kitchen she rummaged around in the cupboards until she found the jar of instant coffee. Since she couldn't find an expiry date on the jar, she shrugged and filled the kettle with water.

"Zipper?" she called out.

She turned around and nearly dropped the jar. "Jesus. Don't sneak up on me like that."

The kid rolled his eyes. "I wasn't sneaking. Not my fault you couldn't hear me, lady."

"Here." She handed him the jar. "Make your coffee the way you like." She watched as he poured a healthy dose of instant coffee into his cup and added hot water from the kettle. "We need to work out this 'lady' thing."

Zipper added cream to his cup. "You're a lady, aren't you?"

"I'd prefer if you called me 'Eileen.'"

"Whatever."

"And I think you should tell me your *real* name."

He glared at her. "My name's Zipper."

"What did your mother name you?" she pressed.

"Zipper."

She couldn't help but laugh. "Yeah, I'm sure. What about a last name?"

"Don't got none."

The look on the kid's face told her the conversation was over.

She sighed. "One day you're going to have to trust someone."

Zipper shrugged. "Can I skateboard outside?"

"Sorry. It's not safe, even in my neighborhood. Someone could see you and talk to the wrong people."

"So I'm gonna stay locked up inside, sleeping on your couch?"

She smiled at him. "First of all, you're not locked up here. We just have to make sure that whoever killed Chen Li doesn't find you. And second, you can sleep in the guest room."

Zipper downed his coffee and set the cup on the counter. "Can I have a shower?"

His question surprised her. "Of course."

Zipper grabbed his backpack from the couch and made his way down the hall.

"I'll show you the guest room first," Eileen said, two steps behind him.

"This one?" he said, opening the first door on the right.

"No! Shut it!"

Zipper slammed the door shut and

cowered against hall wall, his entire body vibrating with fear.

A surge of guilt washed over Eileen. *My God.* Did he think she was going to hit him?

"I'm sorry," she said, releasing a constricted breath. "I didn't mean to yell at you. Just...not that room. The next one."

Zipper followed her to the second door, and when she opened it, she couldn't help but notice the wonder in his eyes as he took in the queen-sized bed and satin duvet cover. She wouldn't have been surprised if he'd let out a 'whoop' and jumped on the bed, but he hung back in the doorway as though afraid to step inside the room.

Damn it, Eileen. Now you've scared the kid. So much for gaining his trust.

"You're saying I get to sleep in here?" he asked, disbelief written all over his face.

"Yup."

"Won't your old man have something to say?"

"Got rid of him a while ago."

Zipper eyed her with a mix of shock and horror. "How'd you do it? Poison? Or did you shoot him?"

She chuckled. "Divorce papers. But between you and me, I thought about the other two."

The corners of Zipper's mouth twitched. The kid almost laughed. Almost.

"You can shower in the bathroom across the hall. Towels are under the sink. There's shampoo, conditioner and soap on the shower ledge. Let me know if you need anything else."

"Okay."

"Oh, one last thing," she said. "Please make sure you put the toilet seat down and aim straight."

Zipper's face turned beet red. "Sure, lady—I mean, Eileen."

He stepped into the bedroom and dropped the backpack on the floor beside the bed. Then he shuffled past her and disappeared into the bathroom.

Eileen returned to the kitchen. She'd make something for breakfast while the kid showered.

* * *

An hour later, Zipper emerged from the bathroom, his face scrubbed clean. Beneath the overgrown bangs and cap, he was what most would call a 'cute kid.' Tanned by exposure to the sun, he had flawless skin and blue eyes. He hadn't matured yet and was lacking the deeper voice that was sure to come, along with facial hair. If the kid didn't have another growth spurt and pack on some muscle, life was going to be very tough on him. Eileen didn't doubt for a minute that he'd return to life on the streets...eventually.

"I'll find you some more clothes later," she said.

He was wearing the clothes she'd given him the night before, his grungy Canucks cap secured on his head almost in defiance of his current state of cleanliness.

"What about mine?"

"I'm not sure they're going to survive being washed and dried."

Zipper shrugged. "These are okay."

She chuckled. "If you give me the cap, I can wash it at least."

"I like it this way."

He sat down at the kitchen table and stuffed a forkful of overcooked scrambled eggs in his mouth. He made a face and swallowed. "This is cold."

"I wasn't expecting your shower to last an hour."

With a shrug, he devoured the eggs, scooping up dried bits with half-burnt toast.

"Better than Dumpster Delight."

She wasn't sure what to say to that.

"You got an iPod?" he asked.

"What's that?"

"Wow. You must be ancient. Don't you know nothing—I mean, *any*thing—about technology?"

"First of all, I'm nowhere near ancient. And I know what I need to know." She studied him for a moment. "How the hell do you know about all these things?"

"I'm not stupid."

"I never said you were. But your lifestyle isn't exactly conducive to learning about technology. Did you go to school?"

"Sometimes. When I was in foster care."

Eileen arched a brow. "When was that?"

"A while ago. Then Pete schooled me."

"Old Pete?"

Zipper nodded. "Him and Alfie looked after me, made sure no one bothered me. Except Pete's dead now."

"He was a good man."

"You knew him too?"

"I did."

He scrunched his eyes and studied her. "Why'd you stop being a cop?"

"It wasn't for me anymore."

"How come? Too old?"

"No, I'm not too old."

"Then how come you quit?"

"Jeez, you're awful nosy."

Zipper cocked his head to one side. "Fair is fair. You know a lot about me. I should know about you since I'm staying here."

The kid was right…to a point.

"I was injured on the job and decided to get out."

The kid eyed her closely. "You don't look injured. You do it for the insurance money?"

She left out a huff. "No, I didn't do it for insurance." She held out her hand. A web of scars trailed down between her thumb and forefinger. "This is why I quit. This is my gun hand."

"What happened? You get shot?"

"No. And I'm not going to discuss it further, so zip the lips, Zipper."

The expression on her face must have been enough because the kid stopped with the questions immediately.

She glanced at the clock. "Bobbi will be over in half an hour to keep you company. I need to go out for a bit."

Zipper scowled and shoved a piece of

bacon in his mouth, chewing noisily. "I don't need a babysitter."

"Good thing then because Bobbi's got enough kids to worry about, and I'm not paying her."

"You afraid I'll steal something while you're out?"

"Will you?"

The kid glanced around. "What's there to steal? The only thing you've got that's worth anything is that TV."

"Then I guess I don't have anything to worry about." She handed him a glass of milk. "Drink up. It might help kick in a growth spurt."

"Aren't you gonna ask me about the shooting?"

Eileen shrugged. "I figure you'll tell me when you're ready."

Zipper drained the glass of milk. "It was too dark out. Plus my mind is…fuzzy."

Eileen refilled her cup of tea before saying, "What do you mean your mind is fuzzy? Were you high? Or drinking?"

"I don't do neither."

She didn't have the energy to correct him. "But you were there, right?"

"Yeah. I saw that Li guy. He was

hanging 'round the alley, waiting for someone."

"Did anyone show up?"

Zipper nodded.

"Where were you?" she asked.

"Crouched behind a Dumpster."

"What did the other person look like?"

Zipper closed his eyes. "I don't know. It was too dark. Then I heard the gun. Everything after that…" He shrugged. "I dropped my skateboard. It made a lot of noise. So I ran."

"Maybe the shooter was already gone."

Zipper shook his head. "I looked over my shoulder. He was chasing me."

"But you got away."

The kid nodded.

"At any time did you see his face?" she prodded.

"I guess so, but every time I try to remember it's like a wall is in front."

Self-preservation, Eileen guessed.

The doorbell rang, and she glanced at her watch. "Bobbi's here. You know, she's a great listener. You should talk to her about this."

Ignoring her, Zipper stood up. "Can I have more milk?"

"Sure. Help yourself."

She headed for the door, but paused to look back at the kid. He was gulping milk straight from the jug. She shuddered—not because she was afraid of germs but because she'd once known another boy who'd done the exact same thing.

Chapter Seven

Family Day was a holiday when families were supposed to get together and do things, but for Eileen it was just another pain-in-the-ass holiday she'd rather forget. Of course, things might be different if she actually *had* a family—unless she counted Bobbi and Larry.

Arriving at the downtown police station, she pulled into the busy parking lot. Constable Larry Norman was waiting for her, his burly arms folded across the chest of his uniform. Thirteen years her senior, he'd protected her ass many times on the job. He once took a bullet for her, which now dangled from a silver chain around her neck.

"Hey, Larry," she said as she stepped

from the car.

His weathered face pulled into an irritated pout. "About time."

"Someone piss in your coffee this morning? Or did they eat the last donut?"

"They assigned me a new rookie a month ago. A *female*."

She laughed. "What's so bad about that? You trained me, and look how good I turned out." She did a pirouette on one heel.

He gave her a wry scowl. "I'm too old for this shit."

"Nah, you're just well seasoned."

"You make me sound like a steak."

She cocked her head. "Am I going to meet your new partner or what?"

"She's late. Again. Probably doing her nails."

Poor Larry. When he'd mentored Eileen, she hadn't been easy on him. But he sure had taught her a lot. He'd taught her how to survive. And vice versa.

"If you could survive me," she said, "you can survive anything."

Larry chuckled. "Well, there is that."

"Anything new on the Li case?"

He shook his head. "We're at a dead end. Pun intended. You get anything from

Zipper?"

"Not yet. He seems to have blocked something he saw. Bobbi's with him now. Maybe she'll have more luck than I did."

"Listen, the kid's whereabouts is between you, me and your friend. No one else can know where he is."

"Got it."

She jumped when a red Mustang swerved into the parking lot and lurched to an abrupt stop three cars away. A woman with cropped black hair and a perfect tan climbed out of the Mustang and hit the auto-lock.

"Your new partner, I presume," Eileen said behind a pasted smile.

"Constable Ava Montoya, 4th Class."

Larry ranked as a 1st Class Constable, with too many years under his belt to count. Montoya had a long way to climb, and based on her petite stature, her rise up the ladder rungs was going to be tougher than the acrylic nails she waved.

"She looks awfully young," Eileen said.

"She turned twenty-nine last fall."

Montoya approached and gave Eileen a nod. "Ma'am."

Eileen winced and opened her mouth to

say something, but Larry cut in. "Constable Montoya, this is Eileen Edwards. She's consulting with us on the Li case."

The woman smiled. "Not *the* Eileen Edwards. I've heard all about you."

"Constable Norman shouldn't tell tales," Eileen said.

"Oh, not from him. You're practically famous at the Academy. Not many police women make it up the ranks like you did."

By "famous" Eileen was pretty sure Montoya meant "old."

"I'm a private investigator now."

"The best in the city," Larry said as he led them up the steps.

Inside the police station she'd once called home, Eileen waved to the officer on the front desk. "Hey, Dutch."

Constable Vigo Ducci—"Dutch" to his friends and "VD" to his enemies—leaned his six-foot-seven-inch frame across the desk and engulfed her in a mammoth hug. "Long time no see, Edwards."

"They've got you on desk duty. What'd you do?"

Dutch held a hand to his mouth as if telling her a secret. "Got shot in the ass."

"Maybe you shouldn't give them such a

big target." She smiled. "Glad to see you're okay. You better be more careful on the job."

Behind her, Larry let out an exasperated huff. "Jesus, Eileen. He didn't get shot on duty. Idiot dropped his gun, shot his *own* ass."

Dutch raised his hands in surrender. "Guilty as charged. But we know whose fault it really was. Don't we, Montoya?"

"So I was in the wrong place at the wrong time." Montoya looked at Eileen. "That wouldn't have happened if some kind soul hadn't left me a fake map to the *women's* locker room, which turned out to be the men's."

"Rookie hazing," Eileen said. "I thought that went out the year I left."

Dutch snorted. "Aw, Edwards, with you gone we need some kind of entertainment."

"Looks like you're the entertainment."

He grinned. "Today's my last day on desk. As of tomorrow I'm fit for duty."

A bearded man in a tan leather jacket rudely shoved between Larry and Eileen, and she stumbled against the wall.

"Constable Martin!" Larry hollered.

The man turned, contempt written all

over his face. "What?"

"You need to apologize to my friend here."

Martin gave Eileen a cursory glance. "Apologies."

When the man disappeared into a back office, Larry said, "Sorry about that, Eileen."

She remembered Rick Martin from her time at VPD. He'd been a reserved man, a family man, though she'd not known him outside of work. His behavior today seemed irrational. Martin wouldn't be the first UC to lose it.

Larry opened the door to his compact office and waited for Eileen and his partner to enter. Then he closed the door.

"So what bee crawled up Martin's ass?" Eileen asked.

"He was undercover for over two years for the GTF," Larry replied.

"Which gang?"

"Demonios de Los Muertos."

"The DLM is highly organized," she said. "They have money *and* a cozy lifestyle."

"Still, Martin only got out two weeks ago," Larry said. "He's not been the same since he went under."

"I heard his wife left him," Montoya said, inspecting her manicure. "Took the kids."

Larry gave Eileen a sideways glance. "He should've gotten out completely, like you did after your UC stint."

Montoya's eyes widened. "You went undercover?"

Eileen shrugged. "Short term. Now, Larry, fill me in on Chen Li. Anything new from forensics?"

"Ballistics say Li was shot with a 9 mm semi-automatic pistol," Larry said. "Distinct striations on the bullet matched a weapon used in several outstanding homicide cases, all with gang connections." He passed her a folder. "This is a copy of everything we've got."

"You swept the alley?"

"Thoroughly."

"I'll look it over one more time."

* * *

Eileen eased the Honda into the alley and parked behind the bookstore. Though the crime scene tape was now completely gone, she could still make out the spot where Chen Li had taken his last breath.

Crimson stained the crevices in the pavement. It would take a heavy downpour to wash away Li's blood. Eventually there'd be no trace of him. It would be as though he'd never existed.

Once out of her car, she skimmed through the reports Larry had given her and surveyed the area. The Dumpster was still in its place behind the restaurant.

Whoever had killed Chen Li had met him behind the restaurant. Was there some significance in that?

According to statements, none of the business owners had witnessed seeing Li or anyone else in the back alley that evening. The restaurant staff had finished their nightly cleanup and had gone home just after midnight. The guy who owned the cigar store had closed at six, as per usual. Crowley's Books had closed around the same time, and Jasper Crowley had gone upstairs to his apartment and heard nothing after that.

She strode toward the Dumpster. Zipper had hidden there the night of the shooting. She crouched down and peered around the side. She could see the doorways to each of the businesses.

But Zipper had been here at night.

The kid had seen Chen Li but not his killer. Why?

She straightened and walked to the back door of Tai-Wan-On. She continued walking past each doorway, rehashing in her mind how someone could approach Li without him drawing his own weapon.

She glanced up. Then she smiled. "No lights."

Above the doors to the tattoo parlor, bookstore and cigar store, the outside light bulbs had been smashed. Only the restaurant's bulb was intact, and that would have made Li the perfect target. The killer would have approached from the far end, sticking to the shadows. He'd lured Li there. Or he had known somehow that Li would be there. Had the killer set up the meet?

She stood in the doorway of the cigar store, aiming an imaginary gun toward the restaurant door. The killer had moved in closer. She took a few steps forward and paused. *Why hadn't Li run?* The blood stain on the ground suggested Li may have moved toward his killer, probably pleading with him for his life. But he hadn't drawn his own weapon, nor had he fled.

Whoever killed Li had taken time to meticulously set up the ambush of an MC president. They were sending a message to the Silver Scorpions.

Now if only she could decipher it.

"So Li's dead or dying, and the killer has the weapon in his hand," she murmured. "Does he ditch it or keep it?"

The answer was obvious. Someone who'd gone through all this trouble to get to Li without being seen would keep the gun and get rid of it later, far away from the scene of the crime.

"The gun's not here."

The killer would have been fully prepared to escape unseen.

Except he hadn't planned on Zipper being here.

When the kid had dropped his skateboard, Li's killer knew he had a witness. Zipper had fled west down the alley. The killer would have followed until the kid had lost him.

Eileen jogged down the alley, studying the numerous exits. A couple of fenced warehouses backed onto the alley. She hesitated when she came to a narrow opening where a fence board was missing.

Zipper would have fit through the opening, but not an average-sized man. The killer must have fled farther down the alley, and that meant the gun could be anywhere. Too bad there were no security cameras in the back alley.

She consulted the map in the folder. There were no security cameras along the street in front of the Tai-Wan-On Restaurant either. She tracked her route on the map until she found the warehouse she was currently standing behind—Malik's Emporium.

Bingo!

The map showed an ATM machine across the street from the front entrance.

Heading back to her car, she called Larry and left a voice message on his cell phone. "You'll need a warrant for the ATM across from Malik's Emporium. It may have caught the killer when he arrived." She listed the address, then added, "As for the gun, I'm sure Li's killer took it with him. Oh, and this was definitely premeditated. He bashed out the lights above the back doors, except for the one outside Tai-Wan-On. Then he waited for Chen Li. Someone wanted the new president of the Silver

Scorpions dead."

Chapter Eight

It was mid-afternoon by the time Eileen arrived home. Bobbi's car was still in the driveway, and she blew out a relieved breath. She'd explained to her friend how important it was that she stay inside with Zipper and not leave the house, but Bobbi had a mind of her own and didn't always listen.

"I'm back," she hollered as she opened the front door. Her voice echoed back, unanswered. "Hello?" Only silence greeted her.

Eileen's smile faded. *Where are they?*

Grabbing a dilapidated umbrella from a hook on the wall, she inched her way into the house, mentally kicking herself for leaving the Ruger in the gun safe.

The living room was empty. So was the kitchen and dining room.

"Bobbi? Zipper?"

Still no answer.

She turned down the hall toward the bedrooms. Something rustled behind the guest room door. "Zipper? You in there? Bobbi?"

Silence.

Reaching for the doorknob, she slowly rotated it. Then she pushed the door open and lunged inside, wielding the umbrella. "Freeze!"

At the same time, Bobbi and Zipper leapt from the floor, screaming and shrieking. Zipper wore headphones that were connected to a cell phone, while Bobbi wore small earbuds that trailed to the stereo on the dresser.

"What the hell—?" Eileen lowered the umbrella.

Panting heavily, Bobbi pulled an earpiece from her ear. "What on earth are you doing? Trying to give me a heart attack?"

"I called you two, multiple times, and no one answered. I thought—oh jeez…" Eileen sat down on the bed. "What in God's name were you two doing?"

"I was playing some relaxation music for Zipper," Bobbi said.

"It was kind of cool," Zipper added.

Eileen ignored him. "And what, pray tell, were you listening to, Bobbi?"

"Zipper's favorite radio station." Bobbi grinned. "We made a deal. I'd listen to his favorite if he listened to one of mine." When Zipper turned away, Bobbi leaned closer and whispered, "Trust."

Eileen wasn't sure if Bobbi meant she'd built trust with the kid or that Eileen should trust her. Either way, she felt like an idiot for nearly assaulting her best friend and a young boy.

Zipper walked past her and flicked the umbrella in her hand. "Not a very good weapon. It's broken."

"Stay in your room," Eileen ordered as she grabbed Bobbi's arm. "I need to talk to my friend."

"Yes, *Ma*." Zipper's smile was laced with scorn. "Want me to take out the trash later too?"

"Actually, that's a great idea," Eileen said without missing a beat. "And I'm sure I have some other chores you can do." She stepped into the hall with Bobbi and closed the door.

"Sorry we freaked you out," Bobbi said.

Eileen took a deep breath. "I shouldn't have overreacted. I need a drink."

Bobbi followed her to the kitchen where Eileen poured a glass of wine. "Want one?"

"Kind of early for that, don't you think?"

"It's noon somewhere." Eileen downed the wine. "I'm waiting for my pulse to return to normal."

"Well, I do have good news for you."

"What?"

"Your house guest is bonding with someone for the first time in a long while."

"I knew you'd be good for him."

Bobbi shook her head. "I wasn't talking about me. He's bonded with *you*."

"Yeah, right. Zipper sees me as a bossy old lady who's keeping him trapped here against his will."

"He knows you're keeping him safe, Eileen. Safer than he's felt in months, maybe years."

"You watch. He'll take off as soon as I turn my back."

"He could've run any time today, but he didn't. That says something. Plus he just called you 'Ma.'"

Eileen explained how she'd managed to get Zipper past the two thugs in the park. "Good thing they bought our mother-son act."

"I think you've bonded with Zipper too."

Eileen clenched her jaw. "I don't think so. I'm simply doing what I was hired to do. Nothing more."

Bobbi patted Eileen's shoulder. "You called him 'Will.'"

"I was trying to get him out of the park—alive."

Her friend sighed. "You can fight this all you want, my friend, but you and Zipper have a connection. He looks up to you. I think you fill each other's voids."

"Some voids can never be filled."

"I know you think that, but maybe they can."

"Don't go giving me one of your destiny and fate sermons. I'm not in the mood. The kid goes to Child Services on Tuesday morning."

Bobbi gaped at her.

"Don't try to guilt me," Eileen said, looking away.

A stubborn silence sizzled in the air.

Finally, her friend said, "I hypnotized Zipper while you were gone."

Eileen's head whipped around. "How did you get him to agree to that?"

"He thought it was a game."

"Did he tell you anything new about the shooting?"

"No. He remembered seeing Chen Li in a doorway and someone approach him, but when I tried to get him to focus on the shooter's face, Zipper shut down." Bobbi chewed her bottom lip for a moment. "There was something else though…"

"What?"

"When he first went under, I asked him simple questions. He refused to tell me his real name. I asked about life on the street, and he became quite agitated."

"You think he's hiding something?"

"I *know* he is," Bobbi said. "And it's more than his birth name. There's something else that scares the crap out of him."

* * *

That evening, Eileen and Zipper ate popcorn and watched an episode of *The*

Walking Dead. Since she hadn't seen the series before, the kid filled her in on the plot.

"I don't get it," she said. "Why not just stay in one of the skyscrapers in a city? If these...uh, zombie—"

"Walkers," Zipper corrected.

"Okay...*walkers* are so stupid then they wouldn't be able to work an elevator or climb that many stairs."

"The survivors don't want to be trapped. They still have to get out and search for food." Zipper shoveled a handful of popcorn into his mouth. "Otherwise they'll starve and die and come back as a walker."

She flinched at a scene where blood and brain matter oozed from a zombie's head. "This show is kind of violent for a kid your age."

"I've seen worse."

Zipper's words cut into her like a knife. "Life on the streets must be tough."

"You gotta fight to survive. Just like Maggie and Glenn and everyone on *The Walking Dead*."

"When did you first—"

"Shh! It's getting real good."

Eileen stifled a retort. The last half hour

of *The Walking Dead* flew by in a haze of decayed body parts as she struggled to get Zipper's words out of her head. *"You gotta fight to survive."*

The phone rang. She picked it up and strolled to the kitchen.

"Dutch got the warrant for the ATM," Larry said.

"Awesome."

"Not so much. Someone got there first."

"What?"

"The camera's recording mechanism was vandalized this afternoon. All the footage from the past week is gone. We have nothing."

"Shit."

"Yeah, except that."

"Whoever did this has planned for everything."

"Keep your eyes open, Eileen. We're not dealing with a sloppy amateur."

After Larry hung up, she mulled over his words. Something was off, but she couldn't put her finger on it.

"It's getting late," she said an hour later to Zipper.

"But I'm not tired."

"Maybe not, but I am. It's almost

midnight."

She waited until he moved from the couch.

"We should check the doors and windows," he reminded her.

Surprised, she gave a nod. "Okay."

He followed her around while she tested the window locks and bolted all the doors. The house was secure, and Zipper seemed relieved.

Setting the alarm, she waved impatiently at the kid. "Off to bed now."

Zipper sauntered down the hall.

Releasing a pent-up breath, she rubbed her forehead as a mild headache bloomed. In the main bathroom, she swallowed a couple of Advil and chased them with lukewarm tap water.

Damn! The kid doesn't have any pajamas.

Entering the room she'd told Zipper was off limits, she ignored the hockey trophies, photographs and science books that lined the shelf on one wall. She tried to wipe clean the vision of the unruffled bed and the scent of stale air. She strode toward the walk-in closet and removed two sets of hockey pajamas from a shelf. Next, she added jeans, t-shirts, sweaters, socks and underwear.

Then she headed for Zipper's room.

"Zipper?" she called. "I have more clothes for you—pajamas."

Opening the bedroom door, she froze at the image before her.

Zipper was sitting on the far edge of the bed, his back to the door. Dressed only in boxers, he was listening to music via headphones while removing a tensor bandage wound tight around his chest. Illuminated by the golden glow from the bedside lamp, a fine web of scars, scabs and oozing sores were scattered across the middle of his back.

Eileen blinked back tears. *Oh my God...*

Zipper must have felt a draft because his head whipped around. "Get out!"

She set the clothes on the dresser by the door. "Your back is infected. Let's get you cleaned up."

Zipper jumped to his feet, his back still facing her. "Leave me alone!"

"Turn around, and sit on the bed."

Zipper shook his head. "You can't see me." His voice trembled.

"I promise I won't hurt you, Zipper. Let me clean those wounds. I won't ask any questions."

She moved closer and tried to touch his shoulder, but he jerked away, and the bandage slid down his side. That's when she caught sight of Zipper's chest. "Zipper, you're—"

"Just leave. Please!"

"How am I supposed to do that?" she asked, softening her voice. "You're in pain."

"I'm used to it."

This simple statement pierced her heart. No child should be "used" to pain.

Eileen closed the door behind her and stood in the hall.

Well, this certainly isn't what I'd expected.

Her mind still processing what she had seen and learned, she went into the main bathroom. The cupboard below the sink held a First Aid kit, and she retrieved it along with a washcloth and set both on the counter. Determination set in, and she went into her bedroom where she selected some extra items to add to those in the bathroom.

She returned to Zipper's door. "Zipper? I've set out a First Aid kit and some other items in the bathroom. If you won't let me help clean those wounds, please at least do it yourself."

No answer.

Shaking her head, she headed for her bedroom and slid between the sheets, her heart heavy and her mind spinning. Almost twenty minutes later she heard the creaking of a door, and an endless sigh of relief escaped her mouth, as though it had been imprisoned in her for months.

At least the kid had taken her advice.

But now that she knew Zipper's secret, what was she supposed to do with it?

"What am I going to do with you, kid?" she whispered.

Chapter Nine

A blaring squall woke Eileen from a fitful sleep. The phone shrilled again.

It's Tuesday. Child Services?

Blinking to bring the call display into focus, she floundered for the phone, nearly knocking over a glass of water. "Hello, Larry. You're up kind of—"

"Is everything okay?"

"It was until you woke me."

"And Zipper is still with you?"

She sat up, immediately awake. "What's going on?"

"Just answer me, Eileen. Is the kid still with you?"

Jumping out of bed, she juggled the phone in her hands as she hurriedly threw on her housecoat and stepped into the hall. She could hear the television in the living room. As she moved closer, she saw Zipper lying on the couch.

"The kid is asleep on my couch."

"Check your doors."

"Larry, I promise you, my house is locked up like a freakin' fortress. Why are you flipping out?"

"Just check them again. Then I'll tell you."

Pressing her lips into a tight line, she walked around the house, jiggling the doors and windows. Nothing had been disturbed during the night.

"The house is secure," she said, standing in the kitchen. "Now what the hell is going on?"

There was a heartbeat of a pause before Larry said, "It's Alfie. Someone beat her up, broke two ribs and one arm, left her for dead."

"Where is she now?"

"Vancouver General."

Eileen took a deep breath. "How bad is she?"

"Pretty bad, Eileen."

Her gaze drifted toward the sleeping

child on her couch. What would Alfie's death do to Zipper? Alfie was the only "family" the kid had left.

"Alfie's going to make it," she said, clenching her jaw. "She's a tough old bird. Now tell me where you are? I'm coming down."

"You know the carwash three blocks from where Chen was killed?"

"Give me the address."

She scribbled down the information, then hung up.

Now what to do about Zipper…

She called Bobbi. "Can you watch Zipper for an hour or so?"

"Sorry, my friend, but I have appointments this morning. I won't be free until suppertime."

"Damn."

"Wish I could help."

"No worries, Bobbi. I'll think of something."

Of course there weren't any other options. She had to bring Zipper with her.

Heading into the living room, she called out, "Zipper, you've got to wake up, kiddo."

Zipper groaned and turned over. "I'm tired."

"You probably are, but I have somewhere I need to be."

"Can't I stay here and sleep?"

"No, regrettably you can't. Come on, get up."

While the kid stumbled back into the guest room, she dressed and made a travel mug of tea and another one of coffee for the road.

When Zipper returned fully dressed in the street clothes she'd washed, she frowned. "Why didn't you wear the clothes I gave you?"

The kid shrugged. "I found these in the dryer. They're clean, right? And they're mine."

"I don't have time to argue, so wear what you want. We have to leave."

"Mmm, smells good," Zipper said, grabbing the coffee.

Eileen hesitated, wondering whether she should mention last night, but thoughts of Alfie lying in a hospital bed made her reconsider. "Come on."

"Where are we going?" Zipper grumbled while following her to the garage.

"I have to meet with Constable Norman. You *have* to stay in the car. Got it?"

"Yeah, yeah, yeah."

She drove like a demon was on her heels, praying that Larry would have good news by the time she arrived at the scene. Alfie was a sweet old soul who'd never hurt a fly.

Please let her be okay.

Eileen shot a sideways glance at Zipper. How the hell she was going to keep news of Alfie's attack a secret? It wasn't as if she could wrap a tensor bandage around that fact and keep it hidden forever.

* * *

The carwash was surrounded by police cars flashing their lights, and Eileen squeezed the car into the only vacant spot, scraping the tires along the curb.

"Parallel park much?" Zipper said with sarcasm.

"I'd like to see you do better, smart-ass. Now scrunch down so no one sees you. And for God's sake, stay in the car."

Zipper pulled the battered hoodie over the hockey cap and slunk down.

"Good," Eileen said. "I won't be long."

Hopping out of the car, she slammed the door shut, stared at Zipper for a second and pushed the auto-lock button on the key fob.

The kid glared back with a disdainful eye roll.

"God, give me patience," she murmured under her breath.

It took her a minute to find Larry. He was huddled beneath the carwash awning with Dutch, Martin and Montoya. Their conversation looked intense. Larry's new partner was arguing over something, while Martin paced impatiently beside them.

She made her way toward the barricade guarded by a couple of rookies and flashed her P.I. credentials at a rookie. "Constable Norman is expecting me."

Larry waved when he noticed her approaching. "Over here, Eileen."

She gave the others a brief nod, then turned to her former partner. "Any news on Alfie?"

"Not yet," Larry said. "Montoya and Dutch are heading to the hospital in case Alfie wakes up."

"Are you sure this is related to…the Li case?"

"Positive. Alfie heard Chen Li's name and Zipper's."

"Were you first on scene?"

"No, I was," Martin cut in.

"What time was that?"

"A little after six-thirty."

Eileen checked her watch. "So almost an hour ago."

"Coagulation suggests she was attacked before dawn," Larry added.

"Who called it in?"

"An anonymous caller. He used the payphone across the street."

She frowned. "You think the caller was involved somehow?"

"Probably just another homeless bum trying to get a reward," Martin said. He jammed his hand into a pocket of his Kevlar vest and withdrew a business card. "Recognize this?"

Eileen didn't need her reading glasses to identify the object. "It's my business card. I gave it to Alfie two days ago." A smear of dried blood on the edge of his sleeve caught her eye. "Did you find it *on* her?"

"On the ground. A few yards from the body."

She clenched her teeth. "The *victim*, Martin."

"Huh?"

"You said 'a few yards from the body.' As if Alfie were dead. She's not."

He lifted his shoulders in a careless shrug. "Would be better if she were. One less homeless person for us to deal with."

She opened her mouth to argue, but Larry grabbed her elbow and directed her away. "Don't give him the satisfaction, Eileen."

"That's one guy who doesn't have a compassionate bone in his body." She took a slow breath and released it. Then she smiled sweetly. "Okay, I'm fine now."

"I know that smile."

She lifted her shoulders. "You know what they say. Karma's a bitch."

"Let it go. Martin might be a first-class ass, but he's a good cop."

She had her doubts.

"Alfie vaguely recollects one assailant," Larry said, "but she was asleep when he attacked her. He knocked her unconscious almost immediately. However, she's positive she heard a man's voice."

"Any foreign accent?"

"She's not sure. But he kept asking her where the kid was. The wounds on her body suggest he...interrogated her for at least a half hour."

"A lot of damage can be done in that

time."

Eileen spied Montoya trying to get Larry's attention. "Looks like you're needed."

When he caught sight of his partner, he released a sigh of resignation. "Take a look around before you go, Eileen. Maybe you'll have better luck than we did."

As she wandered closer to where Alfie had been discovered, she studied the makeshift dwelling the woman had lived in. Alfie had created it from anything salvageable she'd found during her treks down the alleys. Cardboard, plastic, wood and sheets of metal were either duct taped or tied together with rope.

She paused near the entrance, noting the drag marks Alfie's body had made in the gravel as the assailant hauled her from her home. Blood spatter dotted one exterior wall of the carwash. Alfie had been thrown up against that wall. More than once. A crimson trail meandered down the wall, ending in a small blood pool on the ground. This was where Alfie had been left, unconscious and bleeding.

A side alley led to the entrance of the carwash, and Eileen walked the grid, hoping for one lousy clue.

Then she found it.

The clue was both ironic and a little unsettling. It was a paperback titled *Divine Intervention*. The cover was wrinkled and peeling, and she could barely make out a woman with flaming red hair and green eyes standing in front of a burning building. But one thing definitely stood out. The book was bone dry. It hadn't been in the alley long.

"*Divine Intervention*?" she said with a wry smirk. "Perhaps."

The title suggested a religious work, but when she flipped it over to read the back, she discovered it was a paranormal suspense. She hadn't heard of the author before, but then she rarely had time to read anything other than Comic Strip Mama's website. Besides, who read books anymore when there were Kindles and Kobles and i-thingies?

She opened the book to the first page, and what she saw made her smile.

Chapter Ten

Crowley's Books was the only bookstore within a ten-block radius, and from the number of customers browsing the shelves, business was booming. Not only did Crowley's have a wide assortment of popular authors like Jeff Gunhus, Dale Mayer and Gillian Flynn, they had a "Gently Used" bin in the back corner.

Relieved that Bobbi had allowed her to drop Zipper off at her office, Eileen inhaled deeply, and her chest tightened. A coughing fit ensued, one that brought all eyes on her. One young woman rushed over as if she were about to give Eileen CPR.

"I'm fine," Eileen said, choking back another cough.

Why did Bobbi say she loved the smell of print books? The air in the store was dry and stale, and she was sure the books here smelled more like dirt than anything pleasant.

At the far end of the store an elderly man dressed in a stylish navy-blue suit, blush-pink dress shirt and a navy bowtie with pink polka dots waited on a female customer who was returning a hefty bag of books.

"I didn't realize I owned these already," the customer said.

Eileen caught the woman's gaze. They both knew she was lying.

The woman pocketed her refund and immediately went to check out the new releases.

"Jasper Crowley?" Eileen said to the man.

"Who's asking?"

"I'm a private investigator working with the police." She passed him a card.

"Eileen Edwards, huh?" He squinted at her, his gaunt face taking on a gray pallor under the fluorescent lights. "Do I know you?"

"You do now. Mr. Crowley, one of your

books was found near a crime scene." She plucked the paperback from her jacket pocket and set it on the counter. "This one."

Crowley fidgeted with the book, but didn't pick it up. "We can all use a little divine intervention now and then."

"Well, divine me this. The copyright page says 2004, so chances are this was in your 'Gently Used' bin. You've been known to give away books from that bin if they don't sell after a time. You've given some to a homeless boy named Zipper."

"So? It's not a crime to give someone a book."

"No, it's not. And it's not a crime to call 911 when you see an unconscious woman who has obviously been beaten."

Crowley's hand froze.

"Believe me," she continued, "I get not wanting to be involved. But you *are*."

"When I saw the book in the bin, I decided to bring it to Alfie. She was a fan of that author."

"She still is."

Crowley raised his head. "She's alive?"

"As far as I know. She's in the hospital."

Instantly rejuvenated, Crowley waved at a curvaceous brunette arranging books nearby. "Francine, can you watch the counter?" To Eileen, he said, "Would you like some tea, dear?"

"I only have a couple more questions, and I don't want to take you away from your customers."

"Ah, don't worry about that," he said, leading her into the back room. "Francine sells more books than I do. Please, have a seat."

As Crowley filled the kettle and set it on a hotplate, Eileen sat down at the tiny table set for two. "Are you married, Mr. Crowley."

"Only to my work," he said with a grin and a wink. "Francine usually joins me for tea, but I'm afraid she's not my type when it comes to relationships. And by 'not my type,' I mean Francine's not of the right orientation."

"Ah, she's gay."

"No, *I'm* gay." He chuckled. "Your gaydar is on the fritz."

Eileen laughed. "And here I thought you were flirting with me."

"Funny thing about that, Alfie and I used to flirt like teenagers, even though neither of us was interested in the other that way. It was all innocent fun. She used to live a few blocks from here, in a house that's probably been torn down by now. That was years ago, back when she had a family."

"I didn't know that."

Frail shoulders shrugged. "Most people don't. She was one of my first customers when we first opened here in '68. She and her husband, George, were avid readers back then. Good people. It's a crying shame he left her like that."

"Another woman?"

Crowley shook his head. "Cancer. Alfie was never the same after that. Lost the love of her life *and* her love of life. Lost everything else after that, including her home."

"Tell me about this morning."

"I found that book in the bin last night. Francine must have put it there. When I saw the author's name—Cheryl something—I remembered Alfie was a fan. So this morning I got up early so I could drop the book off to Alfie before I opened the store." The old man trembled, and his eyes filled with tears. "I knew something was wrong as soon as I saw her all propped up against the carwash, blood everywhere."

"Did you see anyone else?"

"No. Not until that cop showed up."

Rick Martin.

"Before the officer arrived," she said, "did you see anything else that seemed out of place, like a parked vehicle with its engine running?"

Crowley's brow furrowed in thought. "The only vehicle I saw between here and there was the cop car. It was idling on the side of the road a block away."

Eileen frowned. "What time did you leave to go find Alfie?"

"Just after six."

Something didn't add up. Martin had said he'd found Alfie at 6:30 that morning. So why was his car hanging around the area? As far as she knew, he lived in North Vancouver and had no reason to be in this area—unless Larry had asked him to check something out.

But wouldn't Larry have told me?

Crowley carefully poured a fragrant tea into two fine china teacups on the table. "Do you take cream or sugar?"

"What kind is this?" She inhaled deeply. "It smells heavenly."

"Sakura—cherry blossom—tea."

She took a tentative sip. "It's perfect just like this."

"I agree. My niece, Violet, teaches English in Tokyo. She sends me treats once a month."

Eileen savored another sip then said, "Have you had problems with any of the motorcycle gangs around here?"

"No. They leave me alone. Sometimes one will wander in here, steal a book and then leave."

"Gang members who read. Just what the world needs."

Crowley stared at her for a long moment. "Books can change the way a person thinks, inspire some to change their lives."

"I can see you really love your job, Mr. Crowley."

"Don't you believe in giving someone a second chance?"

"I do. But not everyone deserves one."

"You sound jaded, Miss Edwards."

"Perhaps. But from my experience, people are going to be who they want to be. And no book can change that." She set her empty teacup on the saucer and stood up. "Thank you for your time and the tea, Mr.

Crowley."

"When you see Alfie, can you give her a message from me?"

"Sure."

"Tell her, 'Second chances don't always come 'round. But if one does, grab onto it.'"

* * *

Eileen picked Zipper up at the Mind, Body & Spirit Therapy building where Bobbi worked. The kid was in a foul mood. When they reached her house, the first thing Zipper did was run inside ahead of her, slamming the door in her face.

Stepping inside, Eileen kicked off her boots and tripped over Zipper's skateboard. "Zipper! Put this skateboard in your room!"

"It's not *my* room," came the snarky reply.

"It *is* while you're staying here." A wave of exhaustion flooded her body. "Just put your board away. *Please.*"

The last word seemed to do the trick. The kid jogged toward her, swept the board up and disappeared down the hall.

Eileen sank into the couch, welcoming its comfort. Leaning back, she closed her eyes and allowed her mind to purge itself of the horrors of the day.

When Zipper reappeared minutes later, the kid flopped on the couch next to her and picked up the remote. The house resonated with the sound of a woman's screams.

"Awesome," Zipper said. "There's a horror marathon on tonight."

"Didn't you get enough stimulation watching TV at Bobbi's office?"

"That was so boring. The TV was on a news channel the whole time, and I sat in the waiting room while the secretary watched every move I made."

"It was the safest place I could think of on such short notice."

"I could've gone with you like I did this morning."

"Not where I was going."

"I'm not a wimp, you know."

"I know."

"I can fight back if I need to."

Eileen bit back a comment as a vision of Zipper's tortured flesh came to mind. Should she admit she knew Zipper's secret?

"How's Alfie?"

Her eyes met Zipper's. "What do you mean?"

"I'm not stupid, Eileen. I saw where we went. The carwash? That's where Alfie was staying."

"Why would you think anything happened to her?"

Zipper's eyes rolled dramatically. "Because I saw the cops and the yellow tape."

Eileen flinched. The kid *wasn't* stupid. "Alfie is in the hospital, but I received a message that she's out of surgery."

Thank God Larry had called her when she was on her way to Bobbi's office.

"So she's okay now?" Zipper asked.

"For now. She was badly hurt. We'll know more by tomorrow."

"It's my fault, isn't it?" the kid whispered.

"Of course not."

"You're saying someone just randomly hurt Alfie? I don't believe that."

The kid was far too smart. "You can't control what others do, Zipper. Yes, someone hurt Alfie, but it isn't your fault."

"It is if they were looking for *me*."

"Alfie told them she didn't know where you were, which is true. She doesn't know my address."

Zipper gaped at her. "They can Google it."

"This house is in my ex-husband's name. And my home phone is unlisted."

The kid stretched back and watched her. "So where'd you go after?"

"To talk to someone about a book."

Zipper let out a snort. "Bet you like slutty romance novels with lots of S.E.X."

"I know how to spell." Eileen bit her bottom lip, realizing she sounded just like the kid.

* * *

That evening Eileen and her houseguest dined on Swiss Chalet delivery.

"Don't you ever cook?" Zipper asked between mouthfuls of chicken.

"Not if I can help it."

"I'm a pretty good cook. Maybe I can cook dinner tomorrow night."

Eileen wasn't sure Zipper would still be with her tomorrow, but she didn't have the heart to spoil the boy's calm mood. "Leave me a grocery list, and I'll pick up what you need when I go out. How'd you learn to cook?"

"One of my foster moms taught me."

"Sounds like she was okay. Why'd you leave?"

"She got sick."

Eileen guessed the rest of the story.

"Whose room is that?" Zipper asked, pointing to the first door on the right.

"No one's."

"I don't believe you."

"Don't spoil the mood. Eat your supper before it gets cold."

"If you're asking *me* questions, I should be able to ask you some too."

Eileen bit back a curse. "The room you're referring to was my son's."

"Did he die?"

The air in the room thinned, and Eileen's throat tightened. "Yes."

"His name was Will, wasn't it?"

She blinked. "How did you know?"

"That's what you called me when we were in Stanley Park. How did Will die?"

Eileen staggered to her feet. "That's enough questions for one night. I'm going to have a bath and go to bed early."

"Can we go see Alfie tomorrow?"

How could she deprive the kid of that? "Sure, but only after we've found you a disguise." *And after I've done what I need to do.*

Tomorrow's agenda?

She planned to have a little chat with

Constable Rick Martin.

Chapter Eleven

On Wednesday morning Eileen escorted Zipper inside the bustling police department and made a beeline for Larry's office. He was out following a lead, which was perfectly fine with her.

"Sit here, and don't move from this office," she told Zipper.

"Can I use the computer?"

"You'll never get past the password lock. Listen to your iPhone."

"iPod," the kid corrected.

"I have a headache."

Eileen left the kid in Larry's office and went to the break room where a handful of cops had gathered for the morning ritual.

"Well, isn't this cliché?" she said,

smiling at Dutch. "You're in here eating donuts and coffee."

"Cupcakes, actually." He handed her a napkin. "Try one. The caramel pecan ones are like an orgasm in your mouth."

"I'm not here for a sugar overdose." *Or an orgasm.* "Anyone seen Martin?"

A pimply-faced rookie awkwardly raised a hand. "I think I saw him downstairs shooting up a target."

She strode toward the back stairwell, fighting the urge to look at the box on the counter. She lost. As her willpower swirled down the sink drain, she plucked up a chocolate creation. "One can't hurt."

Dutch's laughter followed her down the stairs.

Prior to entering VPD's indoor gun range, she donned heavy-duty noise reduction ear muffs, a Kevlar vest and safety glasses. She found Rick Martin at the far end of the gun range. Based on the pile of confetti on the ground and the jagged holes in the center of the target he was aiming at, he'd been at it a while.

Martin caught sight of her and slid off his ear muffs. He'd shaved since the last time they'd met, and he wasn't unattractive.

"I think he's dead, Constable," she said, indicating the shredded target.

"What are you doing here, Edwards?"

"I know I'm not a cop anymore, but I still have some privileges."

"Let's see what you've got." He held out a pistol.

"I'm not here to shoot."

"Oh?" Martin shuffled his feet. "Why are you here then?"

"I have a couple of questions regarding yesterday morning."

"Is this about that homeless woman? Because if it is, I already gave my report to Larry."

"Why so indignant? I only want to ask you why you were in that neighborhood to begin with. It's not on your way to work, and you weren't assigned to patrol that part of the city."

Martin leaned against the wall. "You trying to say something?"

"It doesn't make sense to me. Why were you there?"

He pushed away from the wall and brought his face close to hers. "I don't like people prying into my private business."

She touched his arm. "I heard about—"

"What?" he snarled, jumping back a step. "You heard about me, my screw-ups, my wife leaving me? Tell me exactly what you heard, *Ms*. Edwards."

She hesitated. "You're right. I did hear about your wife. And your kids. But I'm not here to judge you."

"Why not? Everyone else is."

The man was hurting. It was as plain as the gaping hole in the target that Rick Martin had an equally large wound in the center of his heart.

"I'm sorry," she said.

A lengthy silence engulfed them.

Finally, she gave him a nod then turned toward the exit.

"Wait!" he hollered. "I was visiting a lady friend. That's why I was near the carwash." He gave her the woman's name and address. "In case you want to ask her."

"As long as she checks out, you have nothing to worry about. I'll let Larry and the others know."

Martin grabbed her arm. "Be careful who you talk to at VPD. Not everyone can be trusted."

"What do you mean?"

"The ATM getting hit was too

coincidental."

"You realize what you're suggesting?"

"We have a mole," they said in unison.

For the first time, Martin laughed. "Go on now. If you have any more questions, text me."

"I'll call instead. *You* can text *me*, but I avoid doing it whenever possible."

His brow shot up. "Who doesn't text nowadays?"

"The same gal who can't seem to operate a TV remote."

Eileen could feel Martin's gaze burning into her back as she removed the vest, muffs and glasses and handed them to the range officer. Taking the stairs two at a time, she made a beeline for Larry's office.

Zipper hovered over the keyboard, no smile, no greeting.

Eileen sighed. "Still trying to figure out his password?"

"I figured *that* out two seconds after you left."

"Jesus Christ, kid." She rushed to Zipper's side. "Shut that down immediately."

"But I'm reading an interesting report on an undercover operation."

Eileen pushed the chair containing Zipper away from the desk. "How do I get it back to the password screen?"

"Hit the 'Escape' key."

"Where the hell is that?"

"My God," the kid drawled. "Don't you know how to use a computer?"

"I prefer to kick it old school." When Zipper's face scrunched in confusion, she said, "I use notepads."

"What about when you were a cop?"

"Larry is the computer nerd." From the corner of her eye, she spotted the "nerd" barreling down the hall toward them. "Quick, shut down Larry's computer."

The kid stared at her for an agonizing moment.

"Please!"

Zipper stood, strode over to the desk, tapped a single key then sauntered back to the chair. "Done."

The office door opened.

"Hey, Larry," Eileen said. "Any news on Alfie? I want to visit her."

"She's awake and stable, but from the sound of things, Alfie doesn't remember much." He flicked a concerned look in Zipper's direction. "I don't think it's a good idea dragging him along with you. Go home, Eileen."

"I will, but I promised Zipper we'd check in on Alfie first."

"If either gang sees Zipper with you, he's—"

"Don't worry, Larry. No one will see him."

* * *

On the way to the hospital, Eileen stopped at a Walmart to pick up a few essential items. Zipper wandered nearby, acting like boredom would lead to certain death. How was it possible that a kid could tune out imminent danger and focus so much on a fleeting moment of discomfort? Oh, the joys of youth.

She studied the kid, trusting her idea would work. By the time she was done with Zipper, not even a former foster parent would recognize the kid.

"Okay," she said. "Let's find a washroom." She removed the items from the bag and ripped off the price tags.

"Aren't those a bit young for you?" the kid asked in a snarky tone.

"They're not for me."

Zipper's brow furrowed in suspicion.

"Who're they for?"

"Who do you think?" She held a pink dress up against the kid.

"Nuh-uh. I'm not wearing that."

"You want to see Alfie?"

"What do you think?"

"I think we have two of the city's deadliest gangs looking for a teenage boy. They won't give a *girl* a second look."

"But—"

"No buts." She stuffed the dress, tights and black shoes into the kid's hands. "You either wear these and get to see Alfie, or you don't wear these, and we go home now."

With limp arms, Zipper plodded toward the washroom entrance. Minutes later, the boy was gone. In his place stood a scowling vision in pink.

"I feel stupid in this dress."

"You look fine." Eileen grimaced. "But you have to take the hockey cap off. It kind of ruins the girl look."

"Maybe it's the dress that's ruining the look." Snark was back with a vengeance.

"Cap off."

Zipper yanked at the Canucks cap, revealing shoulder-length hair tied in a ponytail.

"Put your hair down," Eileen said.

The elastic band snapped from the ponytail to Zipper's wrist. "Happy now?"

Taking slow steps around Zipper, Eileen admired the kid's overall appearance. "Not too dressy. Kind of Sunday church or social gathering style."

"Let's just do this and get it over with."

"Quit sulking, kiddo. Once you see Alfie, you'll forget all about what you're wearing. Besides, you need new clothes—ones that fit you properly."

Blue eyes met hers. "You know, don't you?"

There was no point denying it. "Yes. But we'll talk about *that* later."

Chapter Twelve

Eileen despised hospitals. She hated being in them as a patient and even more as a healthy adult. God only knew what kind of infection she'd pick up just from visiting. She resisted the urge to hold her breath as they entered the Intensive Care Unit, a bustling hub of infections, injuries and illnesses.

A police guard stood outside Alfie's room. The young man gave her a polite nod when she showed him her card. "The victim is awake now."

"Her name's *Alfie*," Zipper snapped.

The officer frowned at Eileen. "Who's the kid?"

"My niece. She's visiting from

Edmonton, and I didn't want to leave her at home alone. She met Alfie last time she visited Vancouver."

The officer opened the door to Alfie's room. "Detectives Norman and Montoya are on their way to take a formal statement. Don't get the woman too riled up."

Eileen shot him a tight smile. "I know how this works."

"Well, you gonna stand in dat doorway all day?" a weak voice called from the bed.

As they entered the room, Eileen took in the battered woman lying in the bed. Alfie's face was a mess of abrasions and welts. A bandage wrapped around her head and a cast on her left arm made her appear all the more fragile.

"Alfie," Zipper said, rushing toward the bed by the window.

The woman raised swollen, bruised eyes, "Who's dat?"

"It's me. Zipper."

"I don't see too well, but I know dat voice. Where you be, honey?"

Eileen stood back, watching the reunion with curiosity. The woman stroked Zipper's hair and cupped the kid's face in her dark hands. Then a hand lightly skimmed

Zipper's attire, pausing at the satin bow at the waist of the dress.

"What you wearin'?" Alfie demanded.

"Take it easy," Eileen said. "Zipper couldn't come in here looking the same as usual. Today Zipper's playing the role of my niece."

"I'm wearing a pink dress. Ew." The way the kid said this made it sound like Eileen had dressed the kid in raw meat.

"How are you feeling, Alfie?" Eileen asked.

"Hurts when I breathe. How do I look?"

"Like you've gone a few rounds in a fight club."

Alfie attempted a grin. "You should see dat other guy. 'Sides, look at dis here bed I got. Food here's not bad either, 'cept you could peel the Jell-O, it's so dry."

"All joking aside, I need to know what happened, what you saw."

Alfie squinted at Zipper. "Didn't tell 'em nothin' about you."

Eileen's jaw clenched. "How many?"

"Two. They was dark-haired and slanty-eyed."

"Asian?"

Alfie shrugged. "Asian, Chinese, Japs—

look all the same to me."

"But definitely not native Indian or Latino."

"Nope. Not dem guys."

"And they wanted to know where Zipper was," Eileen guessed.

Alfie's gaze drifted toward the kid who was holding her hand. "I didn't tell 'em."

"Did they say anything else to you?"

"Naw. But one got a phone call. Heard him talkin'."

"What did you hear?"

Alfie squeezed Zipper's hand. "Said Zipper would be dead by night. But you gonna keep dis kid protected, right?"

"Count on it."

"You do what Miss Eileen tells ya," Alfie said to Zipper. "She say jump, you jump. Ya hear me?"

Zipper kissed Alfie's cheek. "Yes, ma'am."

"You behave now," Alfie rasped. "Miss Eileen's one of the good ones."

"Get well," Eileen said, patting the woman's hand.

Zipper gave Alfie a tentative hug. "I'm sorry this happened to you."

"Ain't your fault, honey."

Zipper blinked back tears, and Eileen knew the kid was carrying the blame regardless of what Alfie said.

"'Fore you go," the woman said, "I did see one thing. Least, I *think* I did."

"What's that?"

"Someone was standin' under a lamp not far away, while dem men beat me."

Eileen's pulse quickened. "You see a face?"

"Naw. He had a coat with a hood on. But he did somethin' strange."

"What?"

Alfie lifted her hand. "He pointed his fingers at me, like dis." She mimicked the actions. "Den he pretended to shoot me, den blew on his finger, like dis." She blew on the top of her index finger. "Kinda like dem old western movies."

Zipper gasped. "That's what I saw too. I remember that now."

"When?" Eileen demanded.

"When that guy was shot in the alley. The guy with the gun did that finger thing after."

A doctor entered the room. He paused when he saw Eileen and Zipper. "I need to take her vitals and check her bandages, but afterward I'd like to talk to you."

As the man approached, she glanced at the photograph on his ID. The face in the photo matched the one before her. *Dr. Michael Iwasaki.*

Pausing in the doorway, she caught the guard's eye and gave a subtle jerk of her head in the doctor's direction.

"He's been cleared by Constable Norman," the young officer said.

"I'm going to call Larry," she said as Zipper followed her into the hall. "Stay here." To the officer guarding the room, she said, "Don't let…my niece out of your sight for a minute. I'll be right back."

Plucking her cell phone from her jacket pocket, she called Larry. "I know you're on your way to the hospital, but I had to tell you this now. One of the guys that attacked Alfie made a phone call to someone. He said Zipper would die tonight. And the guy Zipper saw in the shadows was also there."

"Did Alfie ID anyone?"

"No, she never saw any of them clearly enough."

"Listen, Eileen, I'll be at the hospital in about ten minutes. I'm going to assign a 24-7 guard on you and the kid."

"We're fine, Larry. Once we're back home, I'll set the security—"

"You'll take a guard. No arguments."

She let out an exasperated huff. "Fine."

"One more thing. Keep the kid out of sight from everyone. And I mean *everyone*. We don't want someone to rat out the kid."

She glanced down the hall. "Don't worry. No one will recognize Zipper."

"We can't take any chances. We think there's a mole in the department."

"I know. Rick Martin told me." She gritted her teeth. "Moles and rats. Sounds like an infestation."

"One I plan to exterminate," Larry promised. "We're pulling into the hospital parking lot now. See you shortly."

She headed back to join Zipper. "Sit." She pointed to the chair the guard had vacated. "Give me five minutes with the doctor. Then we're heading home."

When Dr. Iwasaki appeared, Eileen grabbed his arm, leading him a few yards away. "What did you need to discuss?"

"I hate to bring this up," he said, "but we need a next of kin."

"Is Alfie dying?"

"No, she's stable now, and I expect

she'll make a full recovery. However, we have a severe bed shortage. We're keeping her in ICU as a favor to the department. But we'll be releasing her tomorrow afternoon."

"You can't do that! She has nowhere to go except back to the streets. She can't protect herself there. What about infection?"

"I'm sorry, but there's nothing we can do. We have to release her and open the bed, so if you know how to reach any of her family—"

"She doesn't have any family except that kid over there."

"I thought the girl was your niece."

Eileen paced in front of the doctor, realizing her mistake. "She *is* my niece. But she befriended that woman lying in your hospital room. Have you told Alfie this? Maybe she'll contact someone in her family."

"She says she has no one left. Is that true?"

"I've known Alfie for years, but I have no idea if she has any family. I don't even know her last name. So tell me how you're going to put her back on the streets with broken ribs and a broken arm and a face that's been used as a punching bag."

Dr. Iwasaki lifted his shoulders. "I can't do anything more for her. She needs rehabilitation to get full mobility back in her arm. Her family will have to pay for that. Where she goes from here?" He shook his head. "I'm sorry."

Eileen's blood wasn't just boiling, it was curdling. "Great to see my tax money in action."

Deep down, she knew it wasn't Iwasaki's fault. Hospitals all across Canada were hurting. They were overfilled with patients, understaffed by doctors and nurses and competing with the U.S. when it came to salaries.

"Listen," the doctor said, "I'll see if we can keep her for one more night."

She blew out a slow breath. "Thank you. I appreciate that."

"In the meantime, I hope you or the police can track down her family."

She nodded. "We'll do our best."

After he'd left, Eileen waved at Zipper, and they headed for the exit.

"What did the doctor want?" Zipper asked. "He ask you out?"

If Eileen had been drinking coffee, she'd have snorted it out her nose. "What the heck makes you think that?"

"I saw how he was looking at you. You gotta admit, he's pretty hot for an old guy."

"Hot?" Eileen gaped at the kid. She'd barely noticed that the doctor was tall and lean and had deep blue eyes that—*Oh shit.* "No, he didn't ask me out. He wants us to find Alfie's family. You sure she didn't tell you anything? Maybe she has a kid out there? Or siblings?"

"Far as I know, Alfie's on her own. Me and Old Pete were her closest family."

Eileen waited for the heat in her cheeks to die down before she added, "And by the way, Dr. Iwasaki isn't an 'old guy.' He's probably at least five years younger than me."

Zipper snickered. "Cougar."

Before Eileen could react, she heard a familiar voice call her name. Larry headed toward them, followed by Montoya, Dutch and another officer she didn't recognize.

"Hey, Larry." She gave the others a nod. "Montoya. Dutch. Detective…?"

"Cullen O'Brian," the man said, a hint of Irish in his voice. "I'm on loan from Victoria PD."

"I thought we were keeping things

tight," she said to Larry.

"This thing is too big. We needed reinforcements."

"Can we go now?" Zipper said, tugging on Eileen's arm.

Larry's eyes widened. "What the—?"

"This is my niece," Eileen said quickly. "She's visiting from Edmonton. I didn't want to leave her alone at my house."

Montoya smiled. "She'd probably throw a party while you were gone."

Eileen glanced at Zipper. The kid scowled back and picked a hole in the tights.

"If you get bored of your aunt," Dutch said, "I have a daughter around your age. Maybe you and Carrie can go shopping or something." He reached into his pocket. "Eileen, I'll give you my home phone number so your niece can call Carrie."

She plucked the paper from his hands. "We'll see. I think my niece is only here for a few days. Her mother is flighty that way. Just drops her off whenever she feels like it." She was rambling, but she prayed the ruse would hold.

They were nearly out the door, when Dutch hollered, "Eileen! What's your niece's name? I'll tell Carrie to expect a call."

Eileen swallowed hard. "Her name? Uh…"

"Zoe!" the kid beside her called out. "My name's Zoe."

"Zoe?" Eileen exclaimed when she and Zipper were alone in the car.

"I like that name."

"You should've picked something else. It's too close to Zipper."

"Like you said, everyone's looking for a boy." Zipper slouched in the passenger seat. "If I left it up to you, they'd be calling me some wussy girl's name."

"Just because I never had a daughter doesn't mean I don't know good names."

"Yeah? What would you have called me?"

"Exhausting."

Zipper crossed both arms. "Yeah, good name."

Chapter Thirteen

A half hour later, Eileen maneuvered the car into the garage, careful not to hit the tarped vehicle in the second stall and even more careful not to push Zipper. Dealing with the kid was kind of like parking her car. She could go in slow and steady or risk hitting a nerve that would backfire on her. She guessed she'd already hit a few nerves.

"Can I change into jeans?" Zipper asked upon entering the house.

"Go ahead."

When the kid returned to the kitchen where Eileen was heating the kettle, she eyed the kid's clothing choice—a pair of clean jeans and one of Eileen's blouses that had been in the dryer.

"Hope you don't mind," Zipper said.

"Not at all." The blouse looked better on the kid. "I'm making a pot of tea. I can make some coffee if you want."

"Tea's fine."

Surprised, she set a second teacup on a saucer. "It's chamomile tea."

"Whatever. I don't care."

Eileen poured the tea into the cups and carried them into the living room. Zipper predictably flopped onto the couch, so she set a cup down on the coffee table. "I put honey in it."

The kid picked up the cup and took a sip. "It's okay."

Running a tired hand through her hair, Eileen said, "We need to talk, Zipper. I need to know more about you so I can help you."

"I'll share my secrets if you share yours."

"I don't have any secrets."

"Sure you do. We'll both share, one for one. You can go first. Ask me anything except what my real name is."

"This isn't a game, Zipper."

The kid grinned up at her. "My name isn't *Zipper*. And I can tell you're hiding something."

"I told you who I am and what I do. That's all you need to know."

"How did Will die?" the kid asked. "Was it cancer?"

The cup in Eileen's hand rattled against the saucer. "That's none of your business."

"Then I'm none of yours." Zipper leaned back. "Are you ordering pizza again? Because I don't think I can eat—"

"Will was in the wrong place at the wrong time. Do you have any living family?"

"Not that I know. Was Will in a car accident?"

Eileen's heart began to race. "No, it wasn't an accident."

"Hit and run?"

"You could say that. What was your mother's name?"

Zipper shrugged. "Don't know. Did you catch the guy who killed Will?"

The air thickened in the room, and Eileen struggled for a breath. "Yes." She paused for a moment. "How did you get those bruises and marks on your back?"

"Pass."

Eileen shook a finger in front of the kid's face. "We didn't say anything about passes. You have to answer my question. I answered yours."

For the first time since they started the back-and-forth challenge, Zipper seemed ill at ease. "Foster care."

"One of your foster parents beat you?"

"No. The kid in my last family. Jimmy."

"You remember his last name?"

Zipper's brow arched. "Why? So you can report him? I already did that. Not that anyone believed me."

"How can they not believe you? I've seen the scars."

"Jimmy lied. Told everyone I was hurting myself for attention."

Eileen muttered a curse beneath her breath. "Your turn."

"Why'd you quit being a cop?"

"It's...complicated."

"You *have* to answer," Zipper prodded.

"I quit because I lost my focus. I let my partner down."

"Larry, the cop?"

"Yeah."

"And then Will was killed?" Zipper asked.

"Will's death was *my* fault. He should never have been there. I put him in danger."

The words came out in a whoosh of air, clinging to her skin, to every cell in her body, until the bitter air around her became a lead weight reeking of guilt and remorse. "Your question, Zipper."

"Can I see Will's room?"

Gathering her courage, Eileen led Zipper to the hall, where she opened the door to her son's room. "Please don't touch anything."

"I won't."

Zipper moved through the room, admiring the pictures on the wall and the trophies on the shelf. "Will was a good hockey player."

"Will was an *awesome* hockey player."

"He was lucky."

"Why do you say that?"

"He had a real family, even if only for a while."

"I guess he did."

Zipper leaned close to study a family photo by the bed. "You all look happy."

"We were."

"And Will was kinda hot."

A grin crossed Eileen's face before she could stop it. "I guess he was. A few girls were after him. A couple of boys too, I think, although Will was clearly interested in the female gender."

Never in her wildest dreams had she thought she'd be discussing her son like this. It felt strange and foreign and bittersweet to think of him. And so very good, all at the same time.

"Here's my next question," Eileen said. "If another foster home is found for you, will you give it a try?"

"I'd rather live in Alfie's cardboard house."

They both chewed on that for a minute.

Zipper sat down on Will's bed. "Last question for both of us?"

"Sounds good to me." All of these honest revelations were exhausting.

"You go first," the kid said.

"Okay…" Eileen sucked in a deep breath. "Why have you been wrapping your breasts and pretending to be a boy all this time?"

Zipper's gaze was unsteady. "I knew you noticed. What can I say? I thought it would be fun to be a boy."

"The truth, Zipper. You've been passing yourself off as a boy for months."

"Couple of years, actually."

"Why?"

The kid swallowed. "It's safer. When I'm dressed up like a boy, hardly anyone pays me any attention. I come and go, no hassles."

"And as a girl?"

Zipper's mouth quivered. "I get too much attention. Not the good kind. The pimps wanna pimp you out; the druggies wanna mule you. I don't wanna do either. So I dress like I do, and everyone leaves me alone."

"What about your foster parents?"

"They all thought I was a boy. Even Child Services did. I was good at fooling them. Good at not being me."

Eileen resisted the urge to gather the girl into her arms. "The last question is yours."

There should have been relief in Zipper's eyes, but instead Eileen saw only trepidation. She knew that feeling. Nervous expectation. Better to get it over with as soon as possible. "Spit it out, Zipper."

"Well, it seems to me you're an okay person."

"Gee, thanks."

"And I was thinking…since you have an extra room…maybe I could…uh…stay here for a bit. I could help with dinner, since you don't cook. Maybe I could work for your company. I could do office work or answer the phone."

"That's not how these things work, Zipper. You know that. The court decides where you go from here. Not to mention, I'm not a registered foster parent."

"So? You could get registered."

Eileen sat down next to Zipper. "I'm really sorry, kid, but I'm just not the mothering kind."

"You could be. I'd behave. I promise. I'll even go to school."

Eileen patted the girl's hand. "You should go to school regardless of where you live. For now, let's focus on making it through the next few days."

Zipper stood, her face void of emotion. "Can I take a nap in my room?"

"Of course. Are you feeling okay?"

"Just tired."

Eileen watched the girl plod out of Will's room. A second later she heard the guest room door open and close.

She blew out a pent-up breath, thinking of Zipper's request. A knifelike pain twisted through her heart. She wasn't mother material. She'd already had her chance, and she'd blown it.

But still…didn't everyone deserve a second chance? Isn't that what Alfie had said?

She shook her head. *Not me.*

Heading for her bedroom, she paused in front of the guest room door. The heart-wrenching sound of muffled sobs tugged at her soul. Her hand hovered above the doorknob. She shouldn't intrude. She didn't want to give the kid false hope. It was going to be hard enough on Zipper when she had to leave Eileen's place.

Oh, admit it, Eileen. It's going to be hard on you *when she leaves.*

Moving away from the guest room, she entered the sanctuary of her bedroom. She leaned against the closed door and massaged her throbbing temple, while countless questions churned in her mind.

A groan escaped her lips. "What am I going to do with you, kiddo?"

* * *

The doorbell rang just before three-thirty that afternoon.

Eileen checked the security monitor, and her brow wrinkled in surprise when she saw Ava Montoya on her front porch.

"Constable Norman sent me," the woman said via the intercom.

Eileen opened the door. "You're my protection?" The words were out of her mouth before she realized how they'd sound.

Montoya's brow lifted. "I'm a cop. Like you used to be. I'm trained for this."

"Sorry, I didn't mean anything by that. I'm just surprised Larry sent you and not Dutch."

Eileen led Montoya into the living room.

"You guys go back a long way, don't you?" the woman said, sitting on the couch.

"We do."

Montoya sighed. "It's not easy being a cop. Especially a female cop."

"No, it's not. But once you earn their trust, they'll have your back for life."

"I get that. I know I have to prove myself. But sometimes…" Montoya shrugged.

Eileen sensed the woman's uncertainty and vulnerability. "I get it. Sometimes they make it hard. They need to know you've got their backs too. What made you decide to become a cop in the first place?"

"My father always wanted a son,"

Montoya said. "But he was stuck with two daughters instead."

Eileen smiled. "Ah, so you became the 'son' he never had."

"I guess it sounds silly, but I spent the past few years searching for his approval."

"Has he given it?"

"He did. Right before he died."

"That must have given you some sense of relief, knowing he approved of your choice to become a cop."

"Some." Montoya yawned. "Got any coffee? I'm beat."

"I'll make you some."

As Eileen dug out the instant coffee in the kitchen, she heard a door open.

Oh crap! Zipper!

A second later, she heard the kid talking to Montoya. Moving as quickly as possible, she set the mug of coffee on a tray along with cream and sugar for her guest. Then she made a beeline for the living room.

Zipper was still dressed in Eileen's blouse. The kid's eyes flashed at her, demanding to know what was going on.

"I never asked you what Larry told you," Eileen said to Montoya.

"He told me everything."

"So you know that my niece—"

"Isn't your niece but our missing witness," Montoya finished. "Zipper, isn't it?"

The kid nodded.

"Constable Norman sent us some extra protection," Eileen said to Zipper. "This is Constable Montoya."

"Well, you had me fooled. I thought you were a girl." Montoya chuckled. "Though I'm sure you weren't very comfortable in that dress."

Zipper scowled. "I hate dresses."

"Me too."

"Does anyone else know about Zipper?" Eileen asked.

"Just Constables Ducci, Martin and O'Brian. We were told at the same time."

Eileen muffled a curse. *You could've given me a heads-up, Larry.*

"Don't worry, Ms. Edwards. We've all been sworn to secrecy." Montoya smiled at Zipper. "So, Zipper, got any video games?"

"No."

"Hmm, too bad. Most boys are addicted to them."

Zipper rolled her eyes. "Kinda hard to play video games when you live in an alley behind a Dumpster."

"Excuse us for a moment," Eileen said, throwing an arm around the kid's shoulders. "Zipper, I need some help in the kitchen."

When they were out of earshot, she said, "Why are you being so bitchy to her, Zipper? She's nice enough. She's doing her job, watching *your* ass. Remember, I'm the only one who knows you're a girl."

"You didn't tell your other cop buddy?"

"Larry? No. Your gender isn't important right now." *But one day, I'll have to tell him.*

"Fine," Zipper muttered. "I'll be polite to the lady cop."

"I know that's a *huge* stretch for you," she replied with sarcasm, "but I'd appreciate it. Oh, and if you want to play some video games, there are some in Will's room in the cabinet under the TV."

Zipper blinked. "You saying I can go in there to get them?"

"Well, I don't know what games are good, so sure—pick a couple."

The next hour was spent watching Montoya and Zipper blast holes in the bad guys in some SWAT-type shooter game. Though they offered Eileen a third controller, she bowed out. She'd rather shoot a real gun at a paper target. After watching the kid and the cop compete, she knew she wouldn't have stood a chance.

Just before dinner, Larry dropped by.

"I've got a bone to pick with you," Eileen said as she let him inside.

"Sorry about Montoya just showing up. I was going to call you first, but I got distracted by a phone call from Rick Martin. That's where I've been the last hour or so."

"You want to come in for a coffee?"

He shook his head. "No time. Sorry."

"What did Martin want?"

"He used some of his undercover connections to secure a meeting with a full-patch member of the Silver Scorpions."

"Which member?"

"Ray Jackson."

"Alvarez's sergeant at arms? Why would he be willing to talk to you?"

"I have no idea. I'm going to meet Jackson now, and I'd like you to come with me."

Eileen flicked a glance over her shoulder. "What about Zipper?"

"Montoya can watch him. One thing, though. The only way Jackson would agree to a meet is if I promised to keep his name quiet for now. So no one other than you and I will know who exactly we're meeting."

"You aren't telling Montoya?"

"Not yet. Once we've met with Jackson, I'll get everyone else up to speed."

After telling Montoya she had to step out with Larry for an hour or so, Eileen said goodbye to Zipper and headed outside to Larry's vehicle. As she climbed into the passenger seat, she said, "Montoya didn't seem too impressed at being left behind to babysit."

"She'll get over it. I want you with me because you have the best bullshit detector out of anyone I know."

"You think Jackson's going to feed you a bunch of lies?"

"You know how these bikers are. When they want something, they'll give you just enough to satisfy you, nothing more."

Chapter Fourteen

The meeting with Ray Jackson was held in a warehouse downtown. Larry had ordered Dutch, O'Brian and Martin to watch the place to ensure there were no surprise visitors.

When Eileen stepped out of the car, Larry handed her a Kevlar vest. She raised a brow but didn't argue. If there was one thing she knew for certain, a gang member couldn't be trusted.

"If Dutch sees anyone else approach, we're aborting," Larry said while checking the clip and popping it back in his gun. He racked the slide and chambered a round before replacing the pistol in its holster.

"Gee, I thought we were having a quiet

sit-down with Jackson."

"Here's hoping."

The entered the warehouse, with Larry in the lead. Before the door closed, she caught a glimpse of Rick Martin crouched behind the shell of a torched car. He gave her the thumbs-up, and she nodded.

To Larry, she said, "Martin was undercover for a long time. You sure we can trust him?"

"He's a good guy, Eileen."

"He could be the mole. He has the contacts."

Larry's mouth thinned. "But no motive."

"He was once a full-patch member of the Demonios de Los Muertos. A *brother*. They were his family. Don't you think that could be motive?"

"Martin broke all alliances with the DLM once his UC stint was done."

"It would be hard to leave people you consider family," she prodded.

"The mole isn't Martin."

"But can you be sure?"

Larry didn't answer.

The interior of the warehouse was surprisingly clean, though dust and cobwebs hung from the beams above their heads and a musty smell permeated the air. Puddles of water dotted the concrete floor, and the occasional drip could be heard echoing through the building.

In the far corner, Eileen saw a large cubicle with a carpet on the floor and a four-poster bed. "Someone's crashing here?"

Larry grinned. "Porn studio."

Eileen pursed her lips in disgust. "Great. I guess I better watch where I step."

"Stop right there," a man's voice commanded.

Larry raised his hands. "We're here to meet with Ray Jackson."

A black man disengaged his massive frame from the shadows. He reminded Eileen of that actor that had died a few years back, the one who had played the main role in Stephen King's *The Green Mile*.

"Who's the broad?" Jackson asked.

"She's my consultant," Larry said, his hands still raised in front of his chest.

Jackson stared at Eileen. She maintained eye contact until he turned away. With a shrug, he said, "Follow me." He led them up a flight of stairs to an upper level that housed a large office. "Have a seat."

Larry sat down first and shoved a chair

at Eileen. With a casual glance around the office, she sat down on the edge of the chair, prepared to vacate it in a nanosecond if needed.

Jackson placed a cell phone on the desk and tapped it once. "I'm recording our discussion, Constable Norman. For everyone's protection."

"Go right ahead."

"For you to understand fully what I'm going to tell you, I need to start at the beginning. With Pablo."

"His death, you mean."

Jackson nodded. "Pablo always had an issue with stairs. Vertigo or something. When we found him lying at the bottom of the clubhouse stairs nine days ago, we figured it was an accident. But now I'm not so sure."

"Why'd you hide his body?" Larry asked. "An autopsy could have confirmed or disproved your suspicions."

"We needed to keep Pablo's death secret until a couple of sensitive business opportunities were finalized. That autopsy was inconclusive, by the way." Jackson curled his upper lip in disdain. "I suspect the city didn't want to waste much time delving into the death of an MC president."

"And Li? How does he fit into all this?"

"Since Pablo had no sons, no one to hand the reins to, we all voted Chen Li in because we thought that was what the Prez would've wanted. Then someone shot Chen."

"Two dead presidents in less than two weeks," Eileen said. "Not exactly great for morale."

"Who's your new president?" Larry asked.

"No one yet," Jackson said. "The Club agreed to wait until after Chen's funeral before we voted in a new Prez."

"When's that?"

"Tomorrow." Jackson opened a drawer and retrieved a leather-bound book. "I found this yesterday when we were cleaning Pablo's house."

"Destroying evidence, you mean," Eileen muttered.

Jackson ignored her. "This is Pablo's journal. A year ago, he brought in a new prospect that created a shitstorm of controversy. The prospect made full patch a month ago but isn't an executive member. This didn't sit well with the new member.

This journal details several arguments between Pablo and this member, whom Pablo promised would be next in line when he retired. But he had no intention of keeping that promise."

"You think this new member killed Alvarez and then Li for the president's gavel?" Larry asked.

"I don't have any proof, but it makes sense. Especially after you read Pablo's journal. You need to understand something. Unsanctioned hits—especially on one of our own executive members—create chaos and dissention, which isn't good for our Club. Everything we do *must* be for the good of the Club. We have a strict code of ethics, and we follow our Prez, no matter the cost. The only way to remove a president is if he betrays the Club or dies." Jackson gave Eileen a hardened stare and crossed his burly arms. "We *all* need to know the rules. And our place."

"What's the new member's name?"

"Before I tell you, Constable Norman, I need something in return."

Larry glanced at Eileen before saying, "What?"

"I want you cops to push for a full

investigation into Pablo's death."

Larry shrugged. "Easy. Done."

"And if you discover it wasn't an accident, which I believe you will, I want to know immediately. I need to know the truth."

"So you can eliminate the traitor in your midst?"

"So I can let the Club know who's responsible."

Larry rubbed his chin. "I'll have to clear that with my boss."

"Then clear it." Jackson stood, tucking the journal under one arm. "We're done here."

Eileen watched the black giant duck under the doorway. The man merged into the shadows, his footsteps fading with him.

She rubbed sweaty palms on her jeans. "Thank God he didn't ask us to deliver the kid."

"I agree." Larry released a weary sigh. "Come on, Eileen, I'll drop you off at home. Then I'll head over to the Chief Coroner's Office and get them to re-open Alvarez's case."

Chapter Fifteen

It was pitch black outside by the time Larry dropped Eileen off at the bottom of the driveway. Thankfully there was a streetlamp out front to light her way.

Larry rolled down the window and shouted, "Get Montoya up to speed. I'll call her in an hour or so, once I've talked to the coroner."

"Will do." She watched as his car sped away.

Her cell phone rang, and she checked the display. *Don't recognize the number. Probably a damned telemarketer.*

She strode over to the community mailbox two houses down and checked her box. There wasn't much inside—a bunch of flyers, a handful of bills and a menu from Steak and Kegs, a new restaurant that opened up a few blocks away.

Maybe she'd treat Zipper to something other than pizza.

As she made her way up the driveway, Eileen noticed the garage door wasn't closed all the way. There was a two-inch gap along the bottom.

Weird.

When she reached the garage door monitor, she punched in the code. The door groaned and lifted, revealing an empty stall. "What the hell?"

Her Honda Civic was gone.

Racing up the steps that led inside the house, she opened the door. "Constable Montoya? We have a problem. My car's been stolen." She had her cell phone out, but paused. "Constable Montoya?"

No answer.

"Zipper?"

The stillness of the house sent shivers up her spine.

Kicking off her boots, she sprinted into the living room where the TV stood forlornly abandoned, its volume cranked up loud enough to wake the dead. She turned it off.

Her eyes scoured every inch of the room, taking in the toppled chair that rested on its side, the plate of nachos with crusted cheese on the coffee table, the Canucks cap on the kitchen floor and the broken glass on the floor in front of the back door.

"Shit!"

With shaky hands, she called Larry, all the while checking every room in the house. When he didn't answer, she left a message. "Someone broke into my house and took Zipper and your partner and my car. Call me back."

After she hung up, she ran to her bedroom and retrieved her Ruger from the gun safe. Then she headed out to the garage.

No Honda Civic meant she only had one choice.

She yanked back the tarp, exposing a bright red 2010 Camaro. Frank had bought it for Will. Her son had loved that car. She couldn't find it in her heart to sell it, so the Camaro had sat in her garage, hidden from sight under an old tarp. On the first day of every month, Eileen would start the car and sit in it, thinking about her son. Then she'd shut it off, the car never moving an inch.

"No time like the present for a test drive," she muttered as she climbed inside.

The key fob was still in the cup holder where she always left it, and when she started the car, the engine mercifully roared to life.

Eileen sped down the driveway, jumped the curb and hit the street with a soft thud. Instinct told her that whoever took Montoya and the kid would be heading downtown or to the docks, so she drove in the that direction, hoping that she'd spot her Honda Civic along the way. She doubted they were speeding like she was. They wouldn't want to be noticed. Or pulled over.

The Camaro breezed down East Hastings Street as she passed vehicle after vehicle. Two drivers gave her the finger when she cut in front of them.

Why is it that when one needs a cop, they're nowhere to be found?

Part of her yearned to be spotted by police. If they saw her going twenty or more over the speed limit, they'd give chase. And she'd lead them right to the two hostages, if she could figure out where they were being held.

Minutes later, her cell phone rang. She

flipped it open. "Larry?"

"Uh, no…it's Spence?"

It took a second for the name to register. "The kid with the blue lashes and all the facial bling?"

"Yeah. You gave me your card, remember? Told me to call you if I saw Zipper."

Eileen's heart began to race. "Have you seen…him?"

"He's at Liberty Lanes. Two Chinese dudes dragged him inside. He was tied up and gagged."

"But Zipper's alive?"

"Yeah, but I don't think for long."

"Did you see a woman with Zipper?"

"No."

Shit! Had they already eliminated Montoya?

"Listen, Spence, I need you to call 911. Tell them to send Constable Larry Norman and the Emergency Response Team to your location. Tell them about Zipper. Let them know a cop is one of the hostages—Constable Ava Montoya. And Spence? After you make that call, I want you to get the hell out of there. Understand?"

"Yes, ma'am."

"I'm only about five minutes away now." She hung up, confident Spence would carry out her orders.

Her cell phone rang again. This time it was Larry.

"Eileen, we have an APB out for your—"

"I know where they are," she cut in. "Liberty Lanes. I'm about a block away."

"Wait for backup, Eileen. That's an order."

She didn't bother reminding him that she wasn't a cop anymore.

"I'll be there in about fifteen minutes," Larry added. "And we have ERT heading that way too."

She spotted Liberty Lanes ahead. "I'm pulling into the parking lot now."

"Wait there!"

"Gotta go, Larry." She disconnected the call, ignoring the last minute warning Larry was sputtering.

She parked the Camaro, jumped out and ran toward the building. There was a side door on the west side. Parked several yards away was her Honda Civic, the back door still wide open. Leaning against the car was a boy's bike.

Aw, crap! Why don't kids ever listen?

She drew the Ruger from her jacket pocket, checked the clip and crawled beneath a glassless window. With caution, she peeked over the ledge and squinted. She could make out part of the interior of Liberty Lanes. It was a blackened shell, but the floor had been cleared to make room for the skateboarders and others who squatted inside.

Two men sat on some crates. She couldn't see them clearly or hear what they were saying, but they seemed to be in a heated argument over something.

No sign of Montoya, Zipper or Spence.

She sprinted around to the back. A scorched Dumpster sat beneath a large double-wide window that still had its glass, and she tested the Dumpster's integrity before climbing up on top. Wiping the glass with her sleeve, she peered inside.

Zipper!

The girl was bound to a metal post in an area that probably had been the back office at one time. High above her, the ceiling had caved in, letting moonlight inside.

Montoya was nowhere in sight. Had they killed her already, dumped her body?

Spence too?

Eileen checked her cell phone. No messages. She set it to vibrate in case someone called. The last thing she wanted was to alert the kidnappers to her presence.

She eased one side of the window open. With quiet movements, she climbed over the window ledge and slid down to the floor. Crouching, she surveyed the area. Beams, crates and blackened ruins littered the area around Zipper.

She moved closer, staying low. Every now and then, she paused and listened. Moving quickly from one crate to the next, she was now within ten feet of the girl.

A faint sound made her turn.

Ava Montoya stood behind a post. She waved at Eileen once then put a finger to her mouth. Eileen waited for the woman to join her.

"Thank God you got away," Eileen whispered.

"How did you know we were here?"

Didn't Montoya know about Spence? "Someone saw you. They called me."

"And Larry?"

"He's on his way with the ERT. They're probably outside right now."

Montoya glanced toward Zipper. "Let's get the kid out of here."

Eileen nodded.

They made their way toward the girl. When Zipper noticed them, she gave Eileen a look of relief. But that look quickly turned to terror.

"We have company," someone said behind her.

Her stomach roiling, Eileen turned slowly. Two men, one Asian and the other white, had guns aimed at the kid.

"Put down your gun," the Asian said.

Eileen had no choice. She tossed her gun on the ground.

"The police are on their way," Montoya told them.

"Then we'd better hurry," the Asian said. "Tie up the old lady."

Eileen looked at Montoya. "Do you know which of us he's referring to?"

Montoya shrugged. Then she did something shocking. She joined the two men.

Eileen blinked. "What are you doing?"

Montoya pointed a finger at her, then mimicked shooting a gun. Then she blew across her finger. A smile crossed her face as she watched Eileen's reaction.

"I don't understand…"

Montoya's brow arched. "Really? How can that be possible? Larry told me you were bright, one of the best cops he'd known."

"What do you want us to do with her?" the Asian asked Montoya.

Before the woman could answer, a loud voice shouted, "This is the police! Come out with your hands up! You are surrounded."

Eileen took that moment to grab her gun from the ground and fired at the two men. She nicked the Asian, and he went down. In a flash, she threw herself at Zipper, knocking the chair and the girl over. She hauled the girl behind a crate.

"Stay down!" she commanded, ripping the duct tape from Zipper's mouth.

"It was *her*," the kid cried out. "She's the one I saw that night in the alley."

Ava Montoya had killed Chen Li? It didn't make sense.

Eileen fished around in her pocket, cursing under her breath. She didn't have anything sharp enough to cut the girl free.

A bullet ricocheted off a post nearby.

Eileen dragged the chair-bound Zipper closer to the side door. Panting, she looked around for signs of Larry or the ERT. Moving behind some fallen bricks, she tiptoed closer to where she'd last seen Montoya.

"*Psst!*"

She spun on one heel and raised the gun. Someone was crouched near the door. Spence. He pointed to the east side of the building and held up two fingers.

Eileen nodded. Taking a deep breath, she rose swiftly and fired three shots in the direction Spence had indicated. A roar of pain told her she'd hit at least one target. The stream of Chinese indicated which one.

Spence held up a thumb and smiled.

She'd need to have a talk with that kid later.

Out of the corner of her eye, she spotted a shadow moving closer. She took careful aim, and when a head appeared, she pulled the trigger. The Asian's sidekick dropped with a solid thud. *Another one down.*

That left Montoya.

"Montoya!" she shouted. "I don't know what's going on here, but I do know that if you surrender now things will go a lot easier on you."

"I won't be the one surrendering, Ms.

Edwards!"

The woman's voice came from the north side, and Eileen dodged the open spaces to close the gap between them.

"I was abducted along with the kid," Montoya said. "It's not my fault you both were killed by two drug addicts."

Eileen pinpointed the woman's location and tiptoed closer.

Two shots rang out.

"Correction," Montoya said. "Two *dead* drug addicts."

Eileen rounded a corner and came face to face with Ava Montoya.

"Lower your gun," Eileen said.

Montoya smiled. "You first."

"Looks like we have a standoff."

"I wonder how long you'll last. Your hand must be cramping."

Eileen grimaced as excruciating pain rippled through her hand.

"Larry told me you left VPD because of an injury," Montoya continued. "I'm sure it must be excruciating for you to hold that gun, not to mention keep it aimed at me."

"Why are you doing this? You're a cop."

Then it hit her. Montoya was the mole.

Chapter Sixteen

"You're the one leaking information to the Silver Scorpions," Eileen said. "What do you get out of it? Protection? Money?"

Montoya shrugged. "I know who my *real* family is."

Eileen saw Spence moving toward the place she'd left Zipper. *Keep going, kid. Get her out of here!*

"I don't understand why you killed Chen Li," she said, praying she could keep Montoya distracted. "What was he to you?"

"Li was an inconvenience. He got in the way of what I wanted."

"Which was…?"

Montoya's smile grew broader. "My rightful place at the table, as the daughter of one of the most respected leaders of an SSMC chapter."

The gun in Eileen's hand wavered. "What?"

"For someone who's supposed to be so bright, you're awfully stupid."

A million thoughts swarmed Eileen's mind, buzzing away, making it hard for her to concentrate. Then it hit her.

Eileen let out a gasp. "You're Pablo Alvarez's daughter?"

"According to my mother, I am. She listed some other guy as my father on my birth certificate. Eventually she told me the truth." Montoya scowled. "Of course, then I had to prove it to my father."

Everything finally started to make sense.

"My father swore to me that he would make me president when he retired. He even wrote this down in a book."

"Except Alvarez didn't retire. He fell down the stairs and died."

The gun in Montoya's hand wavered. "That was an accident. We were arguing, and he slapped me. All I wanted to do was slap him back so he'd know he couldn't push me around like he had my mother." She smiled again. "You know, his final words to me were to find his journal and bring it to church. You know what 'church' is?"

"A meeting held by executive members within a gang."

"Motorcycle Club," Montoya stated.

"Did the MC advise you to kill Chen Li?"

"Of course not."

Eileen recalled what Ray Jackson had said, that he suspected the new prospect, who was related to Alvarez in some way, was responsible for the hit on Li.

"Ava," she said, softening her voice, "this isn't going to end well for you. One of your MC members is cutting a deal and ratting you out."

"You're lying!"

"Larry and I just talked to him. He has your father's journal."

Montoya took a step back. "That doesn't matter anymore. In fact, I'll use that to secure my position at the head of the table, just as my father planned."

Eileen laughed. "You really think Alvarez meant for you to take over? He was feeding you a bunch of bullshit. The other members knew that. You were a joke to them."

"Shut up!"

"Your father had loyal men at his side. Once they find out who's responsible for their beloved president's death, you'll only be a liability to them. In fact, I doubt you'll live to see another nail appointment."

"That's where you're very wrong. I'll be a hero to the MC. I'll have proven my loyalty by ridding them of you and the brat."

"How can you consider killing a child?"

"Ever hear the story of the scorpion and the frog, Ms. Edwards?" Without waiting for an answer, Montoya said, "A scorpion asks a frog to carry him across a river, but the frog is afraid of being stung. The scorpion says that if he stung the frog, they'd both drown, and what would be the point of that? So the frog agrees. The scorpion climbs on the frog's back, and they set off. Halfway across the river, the scorpion stings the frog. As the frog takes his dying breath, he says to the scorpion, 'Why?' And the scorpion replies, 'It's my nature.'"

"So you're a nasty scorpion who'll sting anyone, even an innocent."

Montoya's mouth curved into a wide smile. "It's my nature."

A flashing light bounced off the wall behind Montoya.

"You forgot an important element of your story," Eileen said.

"What's that?"

"The scorpion is a traitor." Her mouth twitched at the irony. "And when the frog drowns, so does the scorpion."

"Shut the hell—"

Montoya's words were cut short by an ear-piercing bang.

The woman's eyes widened with shock. Disoriented, Montoya glanced around her, then dropped to her knees. Her mouth trembled, and the gun clattered to the concrete floor. A stream of crimson flowed down her chest, and she crumpled backward in a heap, her glazed dead eyes staring blindly up at the ceiling.

"Eileen?" a voice shouted.

Larry.

"Over here," Eileen said, standing up and moving into the open.

He hurried toward her, his gun drawn. "Anyone else here?"

"Two men," she said. "But I think she shot them."

More voices filled the building as the

Emergency Response Team entered through both doors.

"I know the drill, Larry." Eileen handed him the Ruger. "You realize Montoya is the one—"

"I heard enough." He shook his head slowly. "I never would've guessed she was involved in all this."

"She was Alvarez's daughter."

"The family connection Jackson mentioned."

Eileen nodded. "She was arguing with Alvarez when he fell down the stairs."

They moved to Montoya's side, and Larry checked for a pulse. With a shake of his head, he said, "She's gone."

"Where's Zipper?" she asked.

"Outside with a strange kid."

"That would be Spence. If it weren't for him…" She shrugged.

Larry wrapped an arm around her shoulders and led her to the side door. "I'm just glad we got here in time."

"Me too." She peered up at Larry. "You're the one who shot her, aren't you?"

Larry's mouth thinned as he nodded.

"I'm sorry," she said.

"Don't apologize, Eileen. It could've

been you being carried out in a body bag."

"I know. But I also know it's not easy to live with the knowledge that you shot someone you know, someone close to you."

Larry released a heavy sigh. "Let's get out of here."

Outside, she spotted Zipper near an ambulance. A paramedic was trying to take her vitals, but the kid was pushing him away.

"Eileen!" Zipper cried out.

In a blur of motion two arms wrapped around Eileen's waist and squeezed her. "I'd kind of like to breathe here, kiddo."

"I'm so glad you're okay," Zipper said, swiping at the tears that moistened her eyes. "I thought…I—"

"Everything's okay now. We're both fine."

Zipper released her. "I don't know how you found me, but I'm so glad you did. You're my hero."

Eileen cocked her head in Spence's direction. "Spence is the real hero. He's the one who saw you and called me."

Zipper glanced over at the boy, her cheeks tinged with pink.

"Dude," Spence said, eyeing Zipper's

girl clothes. "I'm not sure I should ask…"

"I probably should tell you," Zipper said, blushing, "I'm a girl. For real."

Spence's eyes flared. "What?"

"She dressed as a boy for protection," Eileen said. "Now quit your gabbing. We're all taking a ride down to the station."

"Dibs on riding with you in that Camaro," Spence said, almost drooling over Eileen's car.

"You can both ride with me."

Zipper climbed into the back, while Spence held the door open. He grinned at Eileen. "Can I drive?"

Crossing her arms, she glowered at him. "What do *you* think?"

Spence climbed in back with Zipper.

* * *

"You all right?" Dutch asked when Eileen and her two young protégés arrived at VPD.

"Yeah. Where's Larry?"

"Conference room."

"Follow me," she said to Zipper and Spence.

She led them down the hall and into a large room, where Larry huddled with Martin and O'Brian. Martin sank into a chair and massaged his head, while O'Brien's eyes inflated with shock.

"I'm guessing Larry filled you in on Montoya," she said.

"This is unbelievable," Rick Martin said.

"Which part? That Montoya was Alvarez's daughter? Or that you didn't suspect her?"

"Both."

* * *

The next thirty minutes was spent telling everyone in the crowded room what had transpired from the moment Eileen had been dropped off in her driveway by Larry to the moment Larry had been forced to shoot Montoya. Dutch recorded her statement. Then he interviewed both kids.

Throughout the chaos, Eileen managed to glom onto bits and pieces of information that had been overheard by Spence and Zipper. Ava Montoya had arranged the meeting with Chen on the night he was killed. He hadn't drawn a weapon because he hadn't seen her as a threat. He thought she wanted to hook up on a more personal level. She'd stayed in the shadows, unaware there was an onlooker until she heard the clatter of Zipper's skateboard. Montoya gave chase but the kid lost her. All she knew was that a boy on a skateboard had seen her.

When Eileen had introduced Zipper as her niece, Montoya had accepted it. As far as she knew, the boy they were looking for was long gone. Until Larry told Montoya the truth. She'd called in her men as soon as Eileen had left the house. The kid wasn't even aware she was in trouble until the men showed up at the door—and Montoya let them inside. Zipper recognized them as the men from the park. These were the same men who had attacked Alfie, random criminals that Montoya had on her payroll.

Montoya had staged Eileen's house to look like someone had broken in and kidnapped her, along with Zipper. Her plan was to kill the boy and make it look like she had barely managed to escape. Then she intended to meet with the executive members of the Silver Scorpions and tell them what her father had promised her.

The only time the woman had panicked was when she heard there might be a video of her chasing the kid. To cover her tracks, she ordered her goons to destroy the ATM recording device. However, it appeared one of them had a few brain cells left and had recorded both the conversation where Montoya gave the orders and the deed itself. This was found on the man after paramedics pronounced him dead. While Eileen was giving her statement, the recordings were being logged in as evidence.

Larry contacted Ray Jackson and filled him in. Jackson swore that Zipper was no longer in any danger. There wouldn't be a trial, so witness protection was no longer a necessity.

Eileen held out a hand, and Larry passed her the phone.

"Just so we're clear, Mr. Jackson," she said, "you're saying the Silver Scorpions won't be looking for the kid or seeking vengeance in any way?"

"That's what I'm saying. The kid can go home." Jackson hung up.

She studied Zipper, who was giggling at something Spence was saying. Zipper was looking—and acting—more like the girl she was with every passing hour. It was evident from Spence's smiles and close proximity that he didn't mind the change.

Jackson's words repeated in her head. *"The kid can go home."*

But Zipper had no home except the

street.

Epilogue

A week had passed since the showdown at Liberty Lanes. Life, as Eileen knew it, had returned to 'normal.' VPD had paid for the damages to her home, and she was back to following spouses suspected of adultery and finding lost relatives and the occasional dog. Montoya had been outed as a traitor to the badge—and as Chen Li's murderer, not to mention the two men in the bowling alley. Larry was partnerless, at least for now. Zipper, who was living with a temporary foster family, was seeing Bobbi every day to help deal with the aftermath.

Today, Eileen strode across Stanley Park, searching for a quiet place to sit and think about what she would say at her next meeting. She was drawn toward the Seawall and found herself staring at the Girl in Wetsuit statue. The tide was in, and it surrounded the rock, the perfect backdrop for the statue. She sat down on the Seawall and dangled her legs over the side.

The peaceful quiet didn't last long.

"Did you know that statue was inspired by the Little Mermaid statue in Copenhagen?" a voice said behind her.

"I *did* know that," Eileen said without turning.

"People come from all over just to see this statue."

Eileen turned and grinned at girl standing before her. "You look pretty, Zipper."

"My name's Zoe, remember?"

Eileen chuckled. "Are you ever going to tell me your real name?"

The girl shrugged. "Maybe."

"And you're sure you want to legally change your name to Zoe."

"I'm sure."

"So…Zoe Smith."

The girl scowled. "Smith was the name they gave me when they first put me in foster care. But it'll do."

"And how was foster care this time?"

"The family was okay."

"See? I told you it would be all right. And temporary."

Zoe's smile was radiant. "And I told you they wouldn't turn you down as a foster parent."

Eileen glanced at her watch. "It's almost suppertime, foster-daughter. Our new housekeeper-slash-cook is making spaghetti and meatballs."

"Alfie is really happy living with you."

When the hospital had released Alfie, Eileen knew there was no way the woman would heal living on the street. She'd invited Alfie to stay at her place, a trial run for now to see how Alfie fit in. In exchange for a roof over her head, three meals a day and rehab for her arm, Alfie had agreed to do light housekeeping and cooking.

And Zoe? She was moving into Will's old room. Eileen had packed up her son's personal belongings and now stored the boxes in the garage. One day she'd go through them again and possibly sell or give away the items. But she wasn't ready for that yet. Too many other changes in her life took priority over that task.

She studied Zoe for a long moment, taking in the girl's straightened posture and beaming face. "What about you, Zoe? How do you feel about your new living arrangements?"

"Awesome. Especially now that I won't have to eat pizza four days a week."

Eileen laughed. "Come on, smart-ass."

"Okay, okay." Zoe grabbed Eileen's hand. "Let's go home, *Ma*."

~ * ~

If you enjoyed this book, please consider writing a short review and posting it on your favorite review site. Reviews are very helpful to other readers and are greatly appreciated by authors, especially me. When you post a review, drop me an email and let me know and I may feature part of it on my blog/site. Thank you.

cherylktardif@shaw.ca

Message from the Author

Dear Reader,

This is the first novella in a new Qwickies™ series, and I can't tell you how much I have enjoyed writing about Eileen, Zipper and the others. I have six more titles plotted in this series, and you can expect to see at least one published each year, if not more.

I'm also working on more full-length thrillers. ☺

I truly hope you have enjoyed Eileen and Zipper's journey. Drop me an email, or connect with me on Facebook, Twitter, etc. I love hearing from readers.

Happy reading!

~ Cheryl Kaye Tardif

Works by Cheryl Kaye Tardif

Novels:
SUBMERGED
CHILDREN OF THE FOG
WHALE SONG (Includes WHALE SONG: School Edition [with discussion guide for schools and book clubs] and Large Print edition)
DIVINE INTERVENTION
DIVINE JUSTICE
DIVINE SANCTUARY
THE RIVER
LANCELOT'S LADY

Anthologies or Collections:
SKELETONS IN THE CLOSET & OTHER CREEPY STORIES
WHAT FEARS BECOME
SHADOW MASTERS
A FEAST OF FRIGHTS FROM THE HORROR ZINE
25 YEARS IN THE REARVIEW MIRROR: 52 Authors Look Back

Bundles & Trilogies:
DIVINE TRILOGY
DEADLY DOZEN: 12 Mystery/Thriller Novels
SWEET & SENSUAL: 6 Romance Novels

Qwickie® Novellas:
INFESTATION
EAGLE E.Y.E
E.Y.E. OF THE SCORPION

Short Stories:
DREAM HOUSE
REMOTE CONTROL

Children's Books:
THE ELFLING PRINCESS

Foreign Translations:
VERSUNKEN (German – Submerged)
LES ENFANTS DU BROUILLARD (French - Children of the Fog)
DIVINE: Blick ins Feuer (German - Divine Intervention)
WILDER FLUSS (German - The River)
DES NEBELS KINDER (German - Children of the Fog)
DIE MELODIE DER WALE (German - Whale Song)
DIE MELODIE DER WALE: Schulausgabe (German - Whale Song: School Edition)
LANCELOTS LADY (German - Lancelot's Lady)
GIZEMLI NEHIR (Turkish - The River)

Non-Fiction:
HOW I MADE OVER $42,000 IN 1 MONTH SELLING MY KINDLE eBOOKS

Audio Books:
CHILDREN OF THE FOG
SUBMERGED
DES NEBELS KINDER (German – Children of the Fog)

About the Author

Cheryl Kaye Tardif is an award-winning, international bestselling Canadian suspense author published by various publishers. Some of her most popular novels have been translated into foreign languages. She is best known for CHILDREN OF THE FOG (over 100,000 copies sold worldwide) and WHALE SONG.

When people ask her what she does, Cheryl likes to say, "I kill people off for a living!" You can imagine the looks she gets. Sometimes she'll add, "Fictitiously, of course. I'm a suspense author." Sometimes she won't say anything else.

Inspired by Stephen King, Dean Koontz and others, Cheryl strives to create stories that feel real, characters you'll love or hate, and a pace that will keep you reading.

In 2014, she penned her first "Qwickie" (novella) for Imajin Books™ new imprint, Imajin Qwickies™. *E.Y.E. of the Scorpion* is the first in her E.Y.E. Spy Mystery series.

She is now working on her next thriller.

Booklist raves, "Tardif, already a big hit in Canada…a name to reckon with south of the border."

Cheryl's website: www.cherylktardif.com
Blog: www.cherylktardif.blogspot.com
Twitter: www.twitter.com/cherylktardif
Facebook:
https://www.facebook.com/CherylKayeTardif

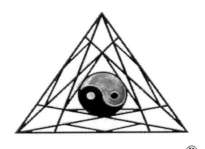

IMAJIN BOOKS®
Quality fiction beyond your wildest dreams

For your next eBook or paperback purchase, please visit:

www.imajinbooks.com

www.imajinbooks.blogspot.com

www.twitter.com/imajinbooks

www.facebook.com/imajinbooks

IMAJIN QWICKIES®
www.ImajinQwickies.com

Made in the USA
San Bernardino, CA
23 January 2018